Louis Sanders studied En[...]
several years in Britain. *De[...]*
and the first in a series set [...]
the Dordogne, was follo[...]
Ignoble Profession is his third. He lives in the Dordogne with his
English wife.

Praise for *Death in the Dordogne* and *The Englishman's Wife*

'An affectionately teasing portrait of hapless British expats out
of their depth. A must-read for anyone thinking of renting a gîte
in France' Michèle Roberts

'A portrayal of rural France very different from the usual sac-
charine tales of expatriate derring-do' *Publishing News*

'Guaranteed to cure you from thinking of a holiday in rural
France' *The Bookseller*

'Complex, well told, and quietly menacing, with a barbed,
decidedly anti-picturesque slant on village life. Discerning readers will queue up for Book Two' *Kirkus Reviews*

'An enjoyable spooky tale which neatly subverts stereotypes of
French provincial life' *Good Book Guide*

'The plot chugs along like a well-looked-after 2CV, making the
trip worth taking' *Time Out*

'This is no jovial cheap-wine depiction of rural France, à la
Peter Mayle, but a subtle, gently misanthropic study of personal
disintegration and the harsh realities of many Brits' French
dream . . . This book will change your mind about retiring
abroad' *Guardian*

'*The Englishman's Wife* simmers with hidden malice and glee. Sanders is particularly good on the dreadful snobbery of ex-pats who ignore the peasantry while buying up their ancestral homes, and still pine for Oxford marmalade' *Glasgow Herald*

'A shrewd, sharp, believable tragicomedy which distils the mushroomy menace of those dark Dordogne woods and posts a "Keep Out" notice for all innocents abroad. A whiff of Patricia Highsmith . . .' *Literary Review*

'Like *Death in the Dordogne*, which would give anyone second thoughts about renting that adorable cottage in rural France, Louis Sanders's silken sequel, *The Englishman's Wife*, is nasty enough to drive property rentals in the Perigord down to a new low. While maintaining the suspense by adroitly shifting his field of focus, Sanders never lets us forget that the real terror comes from within' *New York Times Book Review*

'An original and cautionary tale that resonates with the xenophobic paranoia of the Englishman abroad . . . Bringing a new perspective to "cabin fever", *The Englishman's Wife* is a perceptive account of the life of the expatriate' *Buzz*

'An essential book for anyone planning to buy a house in France . . .' *Living France*

An Ignoble Profession

Louis Sanders

Translated by Michael Woosnam-Mills

Culture 2000 **With the support of the Culture 2000**
programme of the European Union

First published in 2002 under the title
Passe-temps pour les âmes ignobles by Editions Payot & Rivages

First published in this English translation in 2004
by Serpent's Tail, 4 Blackstock Mews, London N4 2BT
website: www.serpentstail.com

Printed by Mackays of Chatham, plc

10 9 8 7 6 5 4 3 2 1

to François

It is my opinion that your detective stories are the normal recreation of snobbish, outdated, life-hating, ignoble minds.

Anthony Shaffer, *Sleuth*

PART ONE

1

Seated in his leather armchair with a glass in his hand, he gazed dolefully at the flames in the fireplace. Three logs lay burning, on top of them a book. The fire flared as the flames licked at the pages. Mechanically, he raised the glass to his lips and took a sip of whisky, barely aware of the tastes and sensations that chased across his palate. Hooked onto the wall at the back of the fireplace, the cast-iron plaque glowered gloomily. The dull relief-work depicted the archangel Gabriel in full armour, appearing to brandish a sword and a crucifix to lash out at anything that might displease him. He towered over a hillock of gray ash, illuminated here and there by the embers below. It occurred to him, for the first time, that he found the image disagreeable, not really part of his world – although for years now he had been looking at it every evening on the assumption that he was perfectly at ease. Confronted by this object which now seemed a constant reminder that everything must be paid for, that nothing can be forgotten.

'Amazing how long a book can take to burn,' he thought. And a good thing too. He pulled a face of disgust, of shame, as certain of the now-blackening pages came back to him. The parts involving him directly. The insistent and, if viewed from outside, almost comical reminders of his social origins, despite the efforts both he and his parents had spent decades making to scrub it all out. He had gone to Eton and Cambridge, he had acquired the accent required to create a new identity – and

3

now, in those two hundred or so pages, he saw himself being tossed back into the world of the petty Leeds shopkeepers who had brought him into it sixty years previously. Perhaps, even, slightly longer ago.

On the logs the covers started curling, as though paper were able to suffer. The flames died down as they ran out of fuel.

He heard a creaking overhead. His wife, no doubt turning over in her sleep up in the bedroom. He didn't need to look at his watch, he knew it was the middle of the night. But he took another sip anyway, and raised his eyes to the chimney-breast with all its pretentious knicknacks, and saw the portrait of himself. True, it was a hideous picture, the whole thing was ridiculous. And all those cruel remarks about his appearance, although that was less serious: he knew he was ugly and it didn't often distress him, he was too old for that. And then there were the rather more cruel passages about the illness of his wife, who was described as a moaning hypochondriac. Which, incidentally, he had on occasion suspected himself. Another creak. Her sleep was restless. Was she perhaps dreaming? He stiffened, apprehensive that she might actually wake and call out for him to bring her a glass of water, a book to cure her sleeplessness, God only knew what else. He hesitated about topping up his glass a third time, then gave in as silently as possible – no clink of bottle on hefty cut-glass crystal. The author of this rubbish must have been here, in this house, because his glasses were described in all their showiness. He had lost count of the people who had crossed his threshold over the months and years. Before Marie's illness, of course. For that had discouraged almost all of them, all these English people living here in cosy exile, like him. With what absurd assuredness had he displayed his wealth, his luxuries, always expensive, often inelegant. He realised it now, and was annoyed with himself for not having noticed, earlier, something so obvious.

It was only when he stood, with some difficulty, to go up to

4

his room that he realised he had had too much to drink. He was puffing. Some said whisky was good for the heart, but he dared not mention it to his doctor for fear of being scoffed at. He moved slowly towards the wide wooden stairs, and leaned on the banister to go up to his room. Behind the second door, his wife slept on. No need to push it ajar: he was only too familiar with the smell of old pillow, of old womanly sweat, of rumpled sheets that would assail him if he took a quick look to see that she was all right. What would this woman's family say if they were to read the book that had been burning downstairs? English-hating, German-loving, unpleasant *grands bourgeois* that they were – though not the petty aristocracy they would have liked to be – and in spite of his wealth, now largely gone but still considerable at the time, they had taken a dim view of the marriage and had made him feel it, from the day he first met them at their large house in the Dordogne, not a château, not a manor, not even a real country house but, appropriately enough, what estate agents call a 'bourgeois residence'.

It was always at mealtimes. They would talk to him of Dunkirk, for example, or the bombing of Caen, whenever mention was made of the war. Just a remark or two in passing. The rest of the time, such subjects were avoided. And Carter gathered that something extremely unpleasant had happened to Uncle André in 1944, 'because,' as they put it, 'of the communists'. And Richard Carter had discovered a whole side to French life he had never suspected. His brother-in-law, the Curé, had refused to say the Mass for his wedding to Marie, on the grounds that . . . well, you see, for a Protestant . . .

In those pages which had claimed his attention for most of the evening, he had had the meagre satisfaction of identifying two people he knew, one quite well, the other distantly. They too had had secrets, which now no longer were.

But worst of all, unimaginable, was the suggestion, between

the lines, of his own guilt in the crime. That old crime which he had committed more than twenty years ago now.

★

Even alone in the silence of the countryside, amid the woods and fields, in this aroma of fresh, damp earth, McGuire had a continuing feeling that all was not quite perfect. Yet he would have been hard put to describe what was missing. An occasional detail would give him an inkling. Riding across the landscape, he would sometimes ponder that it would be nice to see a hedge, like in the days back in Yorkshire when he went hunting and had to jump the obstacle to keep up with the pack. Silly, no doubt, and he would never dare mention it to a soul. Anyway, he felt this explanation wouldn't quite do. He had a list of regrets – smoke in a country pub at seven in the evening, the square of a church tower, the sound of the Sunday papers rustling – which probably amounted to England as a whole. But the England of an era that was gone and which he had tried, somewhat clumsily, to reproduce here in the Dordogne.

Stopping on a hilltop, he was tempted to dismount and ponder awhile as to what life should have been. More money, certainly. So as not to wake up worried in the middle of the night. More comfort here, especially in winter. He would never have believed France could be so cold. He observed his French neighbours' farm from a distance, the farm buildings and their deceptively disorganised surroundings. He had the impression of being on some opposite bank and spying on a perfectly organised world. Families that knew exactly what they were doing, who had never known anything else. He was sure these people had no worries to disturb their profitable, efficient daily round.

Interrupted in these thoughts by the sound of a vehicle on the road, he decided to cut across the field at a trot and move off as quickly as possible. The morning was nearly over now, but it could just as easily have been the end of the afternoon and, strangely, the grayness today was not part of that English scenery that made him vaguely melancholic. Slowing when he reached the edge of the wood, a sharp smacking on the dead leaves told him it had started to rain. Despite himself, he fell once more to thinking of what he had done and what he ought never to have done.

★

'Hitler! Goebbels!'

Lord Bollington was calling his dogs. He heard a faint barking in the distance. It couldn't be either Hitler or Goebbels. He went back up the avenue of lime-trees, leafless at this season, leading to the main gate of the manor. His ankles twisting on the oversized gravel he had ordered to cover the bare earth path, he raised his eyes to the gray of the sky. His head at once started aching horribly, causing him to revise his theory that unblended malt never causes a hangover. Spotting his LandRover a little way off, crashed into the trunk of the third lime-tree along, the events of the night before gradually came back to him. The windscreen was shattered and the bodywork decorated by big black holes where the bullets had hit the vehicle. A few yards away in the grass lay the shotgun. A weapon specially designed for elephant hunting which Lord Bollington took wherever he went, even though the chances of shooting an elephant in the Dordogne were rare. He saw himself at the wheel, driving into the tree in the pitch dark. And the idiotic rage he had felt. He couldn't remember if the windscreen had smashed when he hit the tree, or after. He had got out unhurt – a bit of a miracle in itself – and extracted the elephant gun from underneath the front seat. Then, unsteady and in a fury, he had shot up his own LandRover. He was still wondering why it hadn't blown up.

He heard another gunshot, still just as far away, and turned quickly. Other hunters, people almost like him. It was somehow reassuring to have found, here in the countryside, all these Frenchmen who were perhaps not lords but with whom he felt a surprising affinity. Because they went hunting, they drank too much, and they ate too much. It was better than being in London at any rate, with all those financiers and lawyers talking about what they had been reading lately.

His wife appeared, with a quick, nervous step, calling into his ears:

'Michael, Michael! I've found the phone number of the LandRover garage, if you wanted to ring them up . . .'

'The car can't be repaired.'

'What can we do, then?'

'Get another one.'

The Bollingtons had money.

'Alexandra?'

'Yes?'

'Any beer left?'

'Yes.'

Michael Bollington walked slowly towards his shotgun, surely damaged by the dew. Although it was a top-quality weapon. A third gunshot.

'Alexandra?'

'Yes?'

'What's Marmaduke doing?'

'Reading, I expect. He's in his room, anyway.'

She knew her reply would annoy him, which was why she had hesitated slightly. She could also have said he was pinning butterflies to a card, as he did, and Bollington senior would have been just as annoyed. Marmaduke . . . He was more foreign to him than all the farmers to be heard hidden here in these woods who had just raised an animal with their baying hounds. Lord Bollington turned towards the window of his son's room and thought he indeed saw a silhouette outlined against the cold grey glass. He must have lit a fire and curled up like a cat in his big armchair, doubtless wrapped up in his satin-lined dressing-gown, smoking cigarettes and, as she had said, reading.

Marmaduke had spotted his father in the garden. Letting the curtain drop back he felt a certain apprehension. Seeing the wreck that was his LandRover, Lord Bollington was in a bad mood. A good thing his mother was there to provide the protection he was going to need.

★

Inside, the house was as cold as a barrack-room. And just as gloomy. The sole touch of colour in the cavernous kitchen came from the broken plastic toys scattered over the floor, and the occasional child's drawing nailed to a shelf holding old chipped cups which, in their day, must have cost a bit. Richard Carter called out again. No answer. Not even a bark from the dogs. They must have gone out for a walk. The whole family. But that wasn't like them. There were too many of them. Six kids. And they were in the habit of doing things separately. A group photo showed them together on a bench in the garden, taken last summer by some photographic Gainsborough. Johnny was standing, leaning on the bench where his wife sat with the two oldest, fair boys with feminine features, while the third boy and his two little sisters played in the grass on a large tartan rug.

Richard Carter turned and looked at the laundry and the worn dishcloths drying on lines stretched across the kitchen, above the sink full of dirty crockery, grease-smeared silver cutlery and glasses that had gone grey, their bottoms clouded by wine that no one had bothered to swill out.

The sound of hoofs outside made him turn to the huge, almost opaque window cut into small, regular panes and giving onto a garden lit by an icy sun. Johnny, back from a ride, wearing the brown Barbour jacket that hadn't been washed for months or even years, splashed with mud and torn here and there. For a moment, Richard Carter could not help but admire the man's elegance. Thanks to the education he had been given, he had once been a horseman himself, but had never liked all the rigmarole and hazards that went with it.

Johnny had dismounted and was walking to the stable, removing his hat and wiping his brow with the back of his hand. He paused to look up and observe the sky, hands now in pockets and shoulders back, still unaware that he was being watched from the kitchen window. Richard Carter felt one had to take one's hat off to the unknown author of the book he had burned the night before: the casualness, at once superior and benevolent, that this man gave off was indeed well portrayed. Carter came out into the château courtyard, so as not to appear indiscreet.

Hearing him on the steps, Johnny turned to him with a wave, not really surprised to see him there.

After the ritual eyebrow-raising and polite exchanges, Carter asked if Johnny McGuire's wife wasn't there.

'Laura? Oh, she's in England. With the children.'

'Ah . . .'

'For the holidays. That's all,' he added with a slight smile, having reading Carter's thoughts. 'Financial problems,' he explained, indicating the courtyard with a sweep of the arm.

Carter knew all about the McGuires' financial problems, indeed more than he had thought possible. Thanks to the book. He had read, although without definite proof and certainly not wanting it, that Johnny McGuire had embezzled his wife's money without her knowledge and made some disastrous investments, and had now been reduced to putting the main house up for sale, unable to pay either the heating or the phone bills or, almost, to buy food.

'She's gone back to her family?'

'Yes. I'll show you. Here.' He pointed to a shelf in the kitchen, to a postcard showing a vast eighteenth-century pile across an endless lawn with hundred-year-old trees here and there. 'My mother-in-law's lover's house. He has to open it up to visitors to run it. He gets grants, and he's got his own private quarters – there,' he said, placing his finger on a row of top-floor windows. 'I'm not worried for Laura,' he concluded with a sigh that was followed at once by an amused smile. 'I'm sorry, I've got nothing to offer you. There might be a tea-bag, perhaps. I finished the Nescafé yesterday.'

'It doesn't matter. Not a problem.'

Carter could not help wondering if Laura's leaving had anything to do with having read the book. Johnny hadn't read a thing since leaving his private school and refusing to go to Sandhurst and fulfil the ambitions of his father, a colonel in the Blues and Royals. So he could not know about it. But she – well, perhaps she had read it, and left for England without divulging her real reason: to prepare her revenge in the bosom of her clan, in front of the vast fireplaces of the Derbyshire residence.

'No school at the moment?'

'Yes, but . . .'

Johnny shrugged. This reply confirmed Richard Carter's fears, and he felt increasingly uneasy. He knew he would have to come to the point sooner or later, and could tell Johnny was expecting something from his somewhat puzzled look.

'Are you familiar with a certain Bollington?' asked Carter, who already knew the answer.

'Oh, Bollington . . .' said Johnny in a voice that mixed nonchalance with slight annoyance. 'Yes, I've had dealings with him. Unfortunately,' he added. 'A real shit. Which is exactly what his father said about him.'

'You knew his father, then?'

'My family does. I have some cousins in Yorkshire who live

near the Bollington estate. I've met the father a couple of times. Chap with long grey hair, drunk from morning to night. Like some sort of, oh, Irish poet. Old tweed jackets, that sort of thing. Why do you ask?'

Because Bollington was the third person Carter had recognised in the book, apart from himself and McGuire. Mind you, it was only by piecing together odd bits of gossip that he had reached this conclusion. As well as Bollington's tax evasions, the book also revealed a series of spectacular deeds which ought by rights to have put him away for a number of years.

'You want to start dealing with him? If so, let me advise you not to,' added Johnny McGuire. 'And I speak from experience.'

That too was in the book. Bollington was on the list of McGuire's bad investments. But since the money was purloined in the first place, he was in no position either to get it back or to seek legal redress. And he was not a violent man – unlike Bollington.

'No, no,' Carter replied finally. 'In fact . . . in fact . . .'

There was obviously no point in not saying his real reason for coming.

'I came to talk to you about a book.'

'Oh?'

There. Carter saw he had managed to surprise him.

'What book?'

Carter gave him the title and the name of the author.

'Don't know it. Good book, is it?'

In spite of the polite tone, the conversation was obviously annoying him, and he clearly didn't expect an answer to his question.

'Your wife, er . . . Laura hasn't read it either, she's never heard of it?'

'I haven't a clue.'

'She wouldn't have taken it to England with her, to read on the train?'

McGuire frowned and looked at Carter as though he had gone mad. He was now getting rather irritated by this intrusion. He had been counting on a few hours' sleep before getting drunk in the evening, taking his time over it, in the company of an English friend at the bar in Saint-Jory-de-Chalais.

'How long has Laura been in England?'

'A week. I, er . . . I must say I can't quite understand just where this is all, er . . .'

'Let me explain.'

★

'I'm getting bad vibrations,' said Oriel (whose real name was Norma) on her way back from the goats' enclosure.

She had spoken without stopping to think. Busy at some pointless task in his organic garden, Mark pretended not to have heard. Looking down at her grey socks and sandals, she distract-edly flicked a strand of hair from her forehead.

'Mark . . .'

'Mmm.'

'There's something . . . I don't know . . . Something I'd like to know.'

He made an effort to answer calmly, compassionately almost, or at any rate with great sensitivity.

'Yes?'

'Mark, I've been reading a book.'

No surprise there, then, she spent her life doing that. *Medicine Through Plants, The Planets and Feminine Well-Being, Celtic Wisdom* — then, in the evening, they would discuss them for hours. Or rather, she would hold forth, half drunk, about all the good Saturn did for her womanliness and about the quarters of the moon. In exchange, he was sometimes allowed to watch a football match and even shout at the television if an English club was playing.

13

'Oh yes?' he repeated, stroking his long blond beard to make him look thoughtful. 'And reading this book has got you worried?'

'Mark, when you were an animal rights militant with your operations against laboratories that did vivisection – you know, all that stuff you told me?'

'Yes?'

He had expected some sort of rather boring mutual karmic consolation to follow, but was now starting to feel that something very unpleasant was in the offing.

'You know, you shouldn't believe everything you read in books about militant groups of the kind I belonged to. They're usually financed by the pharmaceutical labs anyway, trying to influence the, er, authorities, because the money, the considerable money they . . .'

'No, it isn't that. Did you ever plant bombs, Mark? Have you ever killed anyone?'

He held her gaze without a word, motionless, looking indeed as if he were about to kill her.

'Mark?'

What was the link between the book she'd just read and her question? She must have been reading some inquiry involving Doctor Gordon, killed by a bomb in his laboratory where he experimented on chimpanzees. But how had she come to wonder if it was he who planted the bomb?

'Mark?'

'Why ask me this ridiculous question? Of course not,' he gabbled. 'I'm, er . . . I believe, er . . . in non-violence.'

He had never spoken so rapidly, and now it was her turn to look at him in puzzlement. Because of his initial silence, he realised, followed by his excited denial that he had ever killed anyone.

'You mentioned a book . . .' he said with a radiant smile that displayed his non-smoker's teeth.

'No, never mind.'

She wheeled away into the restored sheep-shed where she kept her healing crystals and her sticks of incense.

He heard her go upstairs. Then along the landing. She was going to the bathroom. The sound of the key turning in the lock.

He too went into the house, and ran as quietly as he could to the bedroom. No book on the bedside table. He looked under the bed — nothing. Where was she hiding the book? He had noticed she read in the bath. But as far as he remembered, only a novel. It couldn't be that. A novel, which was not her cup of tea, judging by the cover. She was running water for a bath. She shut herself up there for hours on end with her essential oils, her artificial-colouring-free soaps, her beneficial aromas and her relaxing meditation. He walked up and knocked on the door.

'Oriel!'

No answer. Did she think he was going to strangle her, or what?

'Oriel? Meditating?'

'Yes, Mark,' she answered at length.

'May I come in?'

'Not yet. If you don't mind. It's those bad vibrations. I need to find my own space again in the liquid element.'

He returned to the bedroom to have a further look for the book which had perhaps allowed Oriel to guess the truth about him.

★

In one of his trees, Lord Bollington had had built a sort of hunting hide, accessible via a ladder whose wooden rungs were nailed directly into the trunk.

He was posted below the tree, beside him a cage of

ringdoves which he had sent for to Thiviers market that morning. Marmaduke was up in the tree, wearing a tweed jacket and cap, two ammunition bandoliers slung across his plump chest, and a shotgun in his hands.

He had died a thousand deaths going up into the tree, which shook when the wind blew. He felt himself turning crimson; the jacket constricted his shoulders and hampered his movements, and he was not by nature agile. Despite the cold, he was sweating profusely and his shirt stuck to his skin. As he clambered up to the stupid little wooden shack in the tree, confused thoughts added to his fear. He was cross with his mother for not being determined enough to get him out of this 'shooting exercise' imposed on him by his father. It was just an expression of the latter's annoyance at everything his son represented. Then there was the hatred he felt for his father, for this house, for this countryside – though the feeling served to reinforce the basis of most of his thinking.

It took an iron will to keep his eyes fixed only on the tree trunk, not to raise them and especially not to look down at the silhouette of his father below, tiny, glaring up at him with his hands on his hips, his face distorted in a grimace. The gun slung over his shoulders banged into his back at every step, and he was sure he would have a huge bruise. He would stamp his feet and demand that his mother come and minister to him with ointment. But that was still way in the future. When he finally made it up to the hide, he collapsed on the floor, his breathing laboured. He felt he was dangling from a topmast at sea in the middle of a storm. The tree would not stop moving, like some hellish baby's rattle which his father kept shaking in the wind.

He heard a sudden shout:

'Are you asleep?'

No idea how long he had lain there on the boards trying to catch his breath. Although he was only sixteen, Marmaduke got to his feet with all the care of an elderly man getting off a train.

'Gun loaded?'

'Yes.' The answer crept out of his mouth in a terrified murmur.

'Gun loaded?'

'Yes!' he yelled, this time gritting his teeth.

Bollington took a dove from the cage and threw it in the air, with a shout of 'Yours, Marmaduke!' The child shot off both barrels of his gun and the bird exploded in a cloud of white feathers and spatters of blood.

If he missed, he would get a torrent of insults to which he would reply with a series of feeble 'Sorry, Daddy! Sorry, Daddy!' He then considered whether, at this distance, he could hit his father and blow his head off. Difficult with the tiny shot, and anyway it was hard to see how he could pass off the happy event as a hunting accident.

Bollington was getting ready to vomit a few additional insults up at his progeny – who had now missed the second dove – when coming into the drive he spied a LandRover with an army-surplus camouflage tarpaulin, and saw it was Johnny McGuire's. Although not unaware of the justified dislike in which McGuire held him, he was not unduly worried by his turning up because he was constitutionally incapable of the slightest worry. Nevertheless a certain curiosity stirred in him. When he saw a passenger through the narrow windscreen, he did start to wonder if they hadn't come to kill him, with a hunting rifle, for example. As it turned out, immediate events unfolded rather less dramatically.

He saw McGuire get out of the absurd car he had been lent and give him an almost friendly wave. The military vehicle's passenger was a small man of about sixty who walked slowly with his back slightly bent, as though afraid the mud might stain the trousers of his dark blue suit, quite out of keeping with both scenery and season.

'Coming!' called Bollington, abandoning both doves and son in the hide.

Marmaduke was now alone at his station, from where he had not seen the new arrivals and could not understand why the doves had stopped appearing among the branches. He started calling in a small voice, 'Daddy! Daddy!' But there was no reply.

The entrance hall was huge, decorated with large seventeenth-century portraits. Bollington would explain that these were his ancestors, but the book revealed that he had bought them at auction in London, which was more than their rightful owner knew.

Carter and McGuire were admiring the stone staircase that led upstairs when they heard a door open behind them and Bollington's voice barking, 'Johnny! Johnny! Johnny!' with rather forced joviality.

McGuire responded coldly and introduced Carter.

'Ah, I've heard about you,' Bollington replied, 'from Sue Brimmington-Smythe.'

'Mmmm.'

Bollington looked from one to the other as if all of a sudden very surprised to see them. Glancing at his watch, he saw it was half-past-twelve and announced:

'*Apéritif.*'

He led them into a drawing-room with leather armchairs, side-tables and a vast, half-unsprung chesterfield. He went to one of the tables on which were lined up cut-glass crystal decanters of rather tasteless craftsmanship, containing, to judge from the colour of the various liquids, whisky, cognac, port and so on.

'Alexandra not here?' asked McGuire.

'Mass,' replied Bollington, adding, as he turned to Carter, 'we're Catholic.'

He had even been involved in occasional good works, doling out soup for the Secours Catholique in Périgueux – until the day came when he was drunk enough and fed up enough to tell the whole bunch of layabouts to go and clean themselves up and get jobs.

As he was filling three glasses with whisky, without asking his guests if they would prefer something else, he suddenly turned to Carter as though struck by something.

'Of course, the Curé is your brother-in-law, isn't he? Am I right?'

Again, Carter responded with an affirmative grunt, then took the glass Bollington proffered without bothering to say thank you.

'You Catholic?' asked Bollington.

'No.'

'Ah. So just your wife, then?'

'Right.'

'Aha!'

From the tone in which Bollington uttered this last word, he was obviously finding the situation extremely odd, indeed almost incomprehensible. So he turned to McGuire:

'Well, Johnny? What's new? To what do I owe the pleasure of this visit, eh?'

He downed his first whisky straight off and poured himself another, which Carter found reasonably impressive.

'We've got problems.'

'Oh? Don't know that I could be of help because, er . . . I know how you're fixed, and perhaps our friend here too, er . . .'

'I'm afraid, my dear Michael, that you've got the same problems we have, but you don't yet know it.'

Bollington was silent. In the pause that followed, it occurred to him that perhaps Johnny McGuire was threatening him. Thoroughly relishing Bollington's evident confusion, McGuire decided to wait before offering further explanation. But Carter spoiled his pleasure by bluntly announcing:

'It has to do with a book.'

★

He hadn't heard her come out of the bathroom. It was she who had answered the telephone and called, in an annoyed voice, that it was for him. He trotted downstairs and took the still damp receiver. He just had time to catch his wife's eye and register her utter disapproval of the person at the other end.

'Hello? Olson?'

'Speaking.'

'I've got to see you, it's urgent.'

'I don't know if . . .'

'It's very urgent, Olson.'

Mark Olson gave in with a sigh. Before he had time to add another word, he heard Bollington say:

'In fact, it's serious.'

Behind him, he was aware of the presence of his wife, wrapped in her towel, waiting to see if he had the courage to refuse Bollington his services.

'All right. When do you want to see me?'

'As soon as possible.'

'Eleven o'clock tomorrow?'

'Earlier.'

'Not possible. Nine?'

It was Bollington's turn to sigh, before he barked:

'Today. Now. I've got some, er, friends here . . . And we must talk. At once.'

'Right. I'm on my way.'

Olson hung up and paused before turning, to avoid a confrontation with Oriel. Motionless, head down, shoulders slumped. In the end it was she who broke the silence.

'Well?'

'Well, he needs to see me. I have no choice.'

'Ever since we've lived here – he treats you like a servant. He rings, and off you run.'

'I work for him. He pays me.'

'Pfff. You call that being paid?'

Floundering wildly for an answer, Mark could do no better than:

'There's more to life than money.'

Oriel laughed in his face. Mark stared at her in amazement.

'I think you've changed. You used to be not so, er, materialist.'

'My poor Mark.'

'And just what is that supposed to mean?'

'Nothing. Your master's waiting. Off you go.'

With a shrug, Mark spread out his arms in an effort to conceal his anger. But she saw that he had reddened, and not from shame: more from the fury that he controlled increasingly less well. It even crossed his mind to slap her. But he could not because of the game he had been playing for so long, all this idiotic non-violence, human sensitivity and harmony shit. But at this moment he wanted nothing more than to strangle her. She crossed her arms, gave him an arrogant head-to-feet look, then turned on her heel and made for the bedroom.

Despite the downpour, Mark didn't even take the time to put on his ancient anorak. Oriel saw him start the car and go down the drive, great sprays of mud splattering out from under the wheels to muck up the lawn.

Alone in the bedroom, she plucked out a book on the beneficial effects of colours, which could apparently work wonders for her mental, physical and spiritual well-being. For at least the fifteenth time, she read that yellow reflects a highly active aura, that red, if worn, confers a certain sexual power, that blue encourages inspiration, and so on. The consequence of all this wisdom was that she got dressed looking like a parrot and remembered that today was the day of the drawing lesson at Helen Rover's.

When Sue Brimmington-Smythe sold her *auberge*-cum-art-school, Helen Rover began holding drawing lessons there for English artists in the Dordogne, almost exclusively women, gathered around a Brueghel-style model. Classes were held in an old barn which Dave, Helen's partner, had converted into a pottery, painting and other bibs-and-bobs studio.

Oriel had decided to join the group to give free rein to her creativity, even though she felt uneasy there. Everyone was perfectly nice to her, indeed almost tangibly so. But behind her back, she sensed she was a complete laughing-stock. She hadn't wanted to introduce herself by her real name – Norma: so proletarian, not to mention outdated – and had resigned herself to Oriel. But faced with these women, she suspected it was an absurd choice from the barely perceptible pause that preceded it when they called her by name: 'Would you like some tea, er – Oriel?', or 'Could you pass me that cloth, er – Oriel?' But at least she saw other people. And since they had come to live in France, Mark had become a bear.

When she arrived last that day, among these artists, all *Country Life* readers no doubt, she realised that her clothes, too, were absurd.

2

'Lord Bollington is waiting,' fat Albert announced to Mark Olson when he got to the gate of the château.

Mark couldn't help giving the domestic, another rival in the Bollington circle, a lopsided grin, as though he were managing to keep up an appearance of independence. Albert replied with a look which said, 'As for you, I might well kill you one day,' before giving a slight nod and waving to indicate the drive that led up to the large door.

Bollington was in the study with McGuire and another guy of around sixty, obviously tired, whom Olson didn't know. They all seemed somewhat tense and, from the redness of Bollington's cheeks, he could also see they had consumed a not insignificant amount of whisky.

'Come in and take a pew,' said Bollington. 'You know Johnny, and Mr Carter, a . . . er, a neighbour. We want to talk to you about a book.'

The second time that morning. Rather a lot, thought Olson. And at once began to pale.

'You know about it?' This from Carter, who had spotted Olson's reaction.

'Know about what?'

On the arm of the chair he had taken, his hand trembled slightly.

'It's a bit of a – ,' Carter began, ' – a ticklish situation. We're . . .'

'We're in the shit,' Bollington interrupted, coming straight to the point.

And he started laughing.

Carter cleared his throat. McGuire helped himself to more whisky. Together with his hatred for Bollington and the luxury he lived in, the alcohol was contributing to his dizziness, already considerable because of the absurdity of the situation. Never a reader of books, he suddenly saw his whole life being threatened by one.

'Explain, Carter,' ordered Bollington.

'That's just what I was doing,' retorted Carter, piqued. 'As I was saying, it's a novel, in which our, er, little secrets, the most worrying ones, are sort of revealed.'

'What secrets?' asked Olson.

'Read the novel and you'll see,' answered Johnny McGuire, laughing in his turn.

'Hardly the time to make jokes!' Carter rounded on him, for the first time losing his calm.

Still laughing nervously, McGuire could find no better way to calm himself than to drain his whisky at a gulp and pour himself another.

'Hardly the time to get drunk, either,' remarked Bollington, already half drunk himself.

McGuire shrugged and poured, spilling whisky on the mahogany table.

'I have no secret,' Olson announced, making to get up.

'You kidding me?' demanded Bollington at once. 'What about that bomb in the lab, then?'

Olson went white and started to stammer, looking from McGuire to Carter:

'It's blackmail!' he yelled, pointing accusingly at the other three. 'You bunch of bastards! I never killed anyone!'

'Shut up, you moron!' shouted McGuire. 'You heard, we're

all in it, equally. Or just about. There's something for each of us in this book – Bollington, Carter, you, me.'

'Have you all killed someone?'

'I wouldn't go quite that far,' said McGuire, still with the vaguely superior smile. 'But, as Bollington said, we're all in the shit.'

'Go on, Carter,' ordered Bollington.

'When I read the book, I recognised my friend Johnny McGuire here present, and thought one of the other characters would be Mr Bollington– '

'After you'd recognised yourself, don't forget to add,' said Bollington.

'Yes, yes,' replied Carter, now getting increasingly testy.

'And I'll thank you to say *Lord* Bollington.'

Carter raised his eyebrows and looked the other straight in the eye:

'I forgot to tell you that in the book – which you would do well to read – it says your title is a usurped one. Or, more precisely, that your exact title is "lord of the manor", a distinction you apparently bought for a considerable sum.'

Bollington choked and spluttered. McGuire turned away so as not to show he was convulsed with laughter at this marvellous revelation, which partly compensated for the money Bollington had stolen from him. Even Olson cracked a smile. Bollington dropped his glass, the whisky spreading out over the sumptuous Persian rug. Then he took a step towards Carter. The only sober one of the company, Olson jumped to his feet and managed to get his arms around Bollington.

'That's enough, now! Enough!'

Puffing like an ox, Bollington was screaming insults worthy of a genuine lord. In his armchair, Carter crossed his legs with an air of exaggerated calm.

During these actions and exchanges, they all felt they were acting out a farce with themselves as audience. But they were unable to do otherwise, they had no other way to talk to one another. They had spent their whole lives standing around with glasses in their hands, in pubs or at each other's houses, exchanging sallies and witticisms of one kind and another. It was the only language in which they could recognise them-selves. And of course they could also pin the blame on the never-ending sitcoms which they watched on television and which had ended up influencing their behaviour.

And the greater the danger, the stronger the need to come out with sarcastic jokes.

'We won't get anywhere like this,' Carter declared. 'I wanted us to have this little meeting to inform you of the danger which, er, undeniably, is hanging over our heads. Particularly because of the article mentioning the publication, in about six months, of another book of the same kind, a sort of sequel. I'll be perfectly frank with you: this first book does not disclose all my, er, my little peccadilloes, if you take my meaning. And I doubt all has been said about you, my friends. I would like you all to read the novel, and to meet here again in a few days' time. Perhaps, by working together, we can deduce the identity of the author. Then we can decide what measures to take.'

A violent barking rang out across the gardens. Bollington went to the window.

'My wife, coming home from church,' he said. 'Forgive me, my friends, if I do not invite you to stay for lunch.'

★

Despite the french windows and high ceiling, the downstairs room was dark. By one of those optical effects common to 1960s lithographs but in drab colours, the black, white and grey tiles in the hall were laid to make you feel giddy if you looked at the floor. The kind of tiling you could still find, often half-covered in sawdust, in old, unmodernised groceries. They belonged to a world of sad smells, a world which seemed to shrink day by day. He removed his wet coat and hung it beside his wife's. Hers was always dry; she never went out, and her coat had ended up looking like an old blanket, or a piece of soft cloth from which carpet-slippers might be made. The door into the sitting-room opened with the usual rattle of glass. Small panes again – yellow, green, red, opaque. The whole house now seemed to him like a ghastly mish-mash of little panes. With the curtains drawn, the room was plunged in gloom. It wasn't the cleaner's day, and Marie had presumably not left her room. He didn't dare call out for fear of waking her. She was resting. Pehaps reading, propped up on the large embroidered pillows which, she was fond of saying, had been in her family for ever. God knew how many people, he sometimes thought, must have conked out with their head on one of those sacks of elderly feathers, mouth open, struggling to gasp out some last piece of advice about the family fortune.

Carter went over to the fireplace and scattered last night's ashes. It was still too evident that a book had been burned there. Picking up his whisky glass from where he had left it, he took it into the kitchen and dumped it in the middle of the sink. The cleaner would be in tomorrow, and he could use it again this evening without dirtying another glass – how idiotic! The thought surprised him. He was reduced to mimicking his wife's worst traits. He must have been pretty drunk to consign the book to the flames. Now he would have to go out and buy another copy. And read it again, and again, examining the tiniest details to winkle out the identity of this writer who knew them all. The precision with which his own crimes were described made him think that what he had learned about his new-found chums was every bit as accurate.

He had of course written to the French publishers, Les Édi-tions de la Tour Eiffel, expressing both admiration for this most unusual book and a desire to meet the author. Tour Eiffel, which usually published only the memoirs of semi-well-known television personalities, wrote back to say his request would be forwarded. But since he had given a false name, there was no follow-up. Next time he said he was a journalist and wanted to get an interview, even by phone; but the author gave no interviews. He wrote to the translator, care of the publisher, to congratulate him or her on the quality of the work – no reply. He tried directory inquiries, who asked in which *département* of France the person lived. He made a stab at Paris. Nothing that matched the name on the title page. Same thing for the Dordogne. The British publisher of the original book had, he learned, gone out of business, and the book was no longer available in English. None of the press reviews featured a picture of the author, just the book jacket every time, as tasteless as every other book from Tour Eiffel.

He heard movement over his head.

'Marie?'

'Is that you, Richard?'

'Yes, Marie.'

'Where have you been?'

'To see a friend. Anything you'd like me to bring up?'

'No,' she replied, her voice that of the martyr resigned to her fate who seeks to impose nothing too taxing on her entourage.

'Herb tea, perhaps? Not hungry?'

'Come up, Richard. I haven't the strength to keep shouting through the floorboards like this.'

He went up the stairs, knowing what would follow. An hour or more of pretend sympathy, going to fetch all manner of things from the kitchen which she would then let go cold, or make herself vomit up all over the sheets. While he changed them, she would sit in the armchair with a blanket around her and thank him for being so good. She would complain of the cold. Then, it being Sunday, her brother the Curé would come to visit, and he would leave them alone.

★

Bollington was finding it hard to concentrate on the book. He would have liked to ask his wife to read it for him and give him a brief résumé, but he realised that was a non-starter. Finally he reached a bit where he recognised himself, and all at once found he was reading avidly. He turned pale and almost felt afraid, though not at all because of the author's skill with the techniques of suspense. The passage recounted how his wife, an Irish Catholic from a halfway presentable family, had, in a fit of youthful enthusiasm, got involved − albeit only vaguely, but enough to send her to prison had she been caught − with IRA members in Cork. After her continual begging, he had lent his Gibraltar-based yacht to bring arms into Ireland − a notion he had not found displeasing; it had brought back films he'd seen in his childhood. And even though he was English, Alexandra had persuaded him that he was first and foremost a Catholic. To his objection that he was not an Irish Republican, she retorted something he could no longer recall. They had since had occasion to regret the adventure, and evidently it wasn't over yet.

Carter certainly couldn't know the whole story, and in fact neither could McGuire, even though he was of Scots Presbyterian stock and would no doubt have something to say about it. No, this was not his main worry. Olson knew, of course, and with good reason.

★

Johnny McGuire was back in the icy manor. After much difficulty lighting the wood stove in the room normally reserved for watching television, he lay on a tatty old sofa and immersed himself in the same activity as Bollington. When he got to the bits about Bollington, whom he recognised at once, he burst out laughing, feeling more delight than from any book he had ever read before. He had, it was true, read very few, and he decided he would devote more time to cultivating his literary education. The pages describing him seemed, well, perhaps not so well written, a little lacking in competence. But despite the exaggeration, the caricature almost, it was, quite clearly, him. The details of his shameful little swindle, quite accurately described despite the odd error or slight inexactitude, could indeed have an undesirable effect on his future. He wondered what Carter would think of him. Mind you, from that point of view at least, everything revealed about Carter was reassuring. Olson, now, if he had in fact caused the death of some scientist . . . McGuire couldn't suppress a smile when he reached a description, even if a trifle cruel, of Carter's physical imperfections. These thoughts helped take his mind off the object of the exercise – namely, to work out who could know about all these episodes in his past.

★

'You're the fourth person who's asked this morning. I think I may have one left but I'm not quite sure. I'll have to re-order. Haven't I already sold you a copy?' The village newsagent-cum-bookseller frowned, as though his shop had become the scene of something a little troubling, perhaps even morally suspect.

'I lent it to someone and they didn't give it back,' replied Carter while the shopkeeper, a man of about forty with a moustache and a grey shopcoat like in an old movie, scanned his shelves.

Carter was starting to find the olde-worlde aspect of some Dordogne shops a little tedious.

'Selling well, is it, this book?' he asked, although he already knew the answer.

'Funnily enough,' the shopkeeper replied – his voice, too,

sounded like one in an old movie – 'it's mostly English people from around here asking for it, people like yourself, if you take my meaning.'

He ended with a smile, as though what he had just said was in some way funny. Carter limited his reply to a series of grunts.

There was still one copy left on the shelf. Carter made off with it reluctantly, to spend the next few days composing a critical review of a very particular kind of book.

★

Olson looked for Oriel for a good half-hour before giving up. He was now in no doubt that the book she was reading was the one that had been brought up by that bastard Bollington, the idiot McGuire, and that shrunken little pedant whom he had immediately classed as a reactionary snob. He went straight to the bathroom and found the book he was looking for, swollen up like a damp sponge. There he had been, only a few hours earlier, searching all over the place for some stupid essay or other, and it finally turned out to be just this everyday novel completely lacking in spiritual, so to speak, content. The pages had gone wavy, the print smudged in places. He checked the number of pages and saw he was in for a doorstopper. It was with a sigh of relief that he settled by the fireplace on the sofa, draped with some African material.

★

When he got back home, Carter ran into his brother-in-law, who was just leaving. They greeted each other reluctantly. The Curé bent forward – a movement Carter thought rather over-done: was it a sarcastically unctuous bow, or just another way this man of God had of showing that he was a good ten centi-metres taller than his host? The crew-cut, the greying temples,

31

the square jaw, the straight nose and the broad shoulders could let him pass for a military padré or, even more likely, some brute out of the Foreign Legion. The smile, however, a little too syrupy, was not a military one. But Carter knew his brother-in-law had not always been all sweetness and light. As a young man he had been an active militant in extreme right fundamentalist movements, a kind of hysteria which Carter found very French and especially distasteful. He had spent more than one dinner listening to the man pontificating on the mysteries of the Celtic race and on Mother Church, Marie nodding her head with that beatific smile at all the bloody idiocies her baby brother trotted out. Then he would move on to the War, to Pétain, and to right-wing movements such as *Action Française*.

'Reading?' inquired the priest, indicating the plastic bag under Carter's arm, the cover of the book partly visible.

Carter looked up to scrutinise his brother-in-law's face. If he had read the book, he would recognise the colours and some of the letters showing through the white plastic, which was as see-through as a wet T-shirt. He looked for something to say, but finally remained silent and took off his coat with slow, deliberate care. He was beginning to feel weary, and had no time to waste on small-talk with this bastard who in any case detested him and who was now going to pry into his past.

'Marie is in her room, I suppose?' asked Carter, as if addressing the housemaid.

Pierre, Marie's brother and priest, could not avoid raising his eyebrows, with a slight backward jerk. Busy hanging his coat on its hook, Carter did not notice.

'Good day to you,' said Carter. Then, with an inward smile due to his impatience with everything today, he added, 'Father.'

He had never permitted himself such an impertinence before. The priest sailed through the door without another word.

Carter felt like screaming with laughter, like rushing into his wife's sickroom and yelling into her ears, 'How about that? That bastard brother of yours, I've never been so rude to the fucker before. Always sneering at me. He makes me sorry I married you.'

But instead he just called out, as he always did when he came into the room:

'Marie? All right?'

And a weak little voice answered through the ceiling, as though from heaven, as though finally in the hereafter.

'Anything you'd like, Marie?'

'No, Richard, nothing. I've had a visit from my brother.'

'Yes, I know. We met at the door.'

'Where have you been?'

'Shopping. Rest, Marie. Everything's fine.'

'Richard, what are you doing?'

'Reading.'

★

Olson, who had finished his reading, pondered that now the time was no longer for literature but for reckonings, for assessments, for estimates, for bottom lines. He was clearly recognisable in this nasty little book – Oriel had not been mistaken. And, incidentally, where was she? He realised he didn't trust her at all, and wouldn't be surprised if she had gone to report him to the police. For the murder of Doctor Gordon. Bollington knew about it. But who else could also have known about the affairs of this crappy, phony little lord? And about the other little creep, and about McGuire? One thing was obvious: the author was local, lived in the Dordogne, and was English. It was the area that connected them all, that had become their common ground, the tree-covered hillsides, the old yellow stone houses, the scorching summers, the incessant spring rains, the unending winters, the parties, the alcohol. It made up an English way of lying, of falsehood, of crime.

Animal rights . . . He couldn't believe he had got into such a fucking mess over something so bloody stupid. And Oriel still not back yet. He decided — but was it really a decision? — that when she got back he would make one of those scenes he could do so well, like when she couldn't manage to stop smoking or when tofu wasn't exactly what he wanted. In the meantime, he needed to see the others again. He smiled when he recalled, somewhere from the middle of the book, the rather accurate description of Bollington. And he indeed had learned a few things. He knew Bollington had fooled around with the IRA under the influence of his wife. Because it was thanks to it that he, Olson, had been able to get out of the Gordon business. The bomb had been supplied by IRA bomb-makers based in London. The connections between various active terrorist groups — or, as they were called, 'destabilising elements' — had allowed Olson to leave England under a false name aboard the very same Bollington yacht which had been used to bring weapons into Ireland.

Carter, he had never heard of before. But after reading chapter three, he understood rather better the look that had come over him when Bollington said that they, at any rate, hadn't killed anyone. The opposite was more than hinted at, and towards the end there was promise of a further book concerning Carter's part in a poisoning some twenty years earlier. When they had all met at Bollington's, the others had surely not yet known. Nonetheless, it was difficult to think of someone who knew him, Olson, and also Bollington and Carter and McGuire. Even if what the book said McGuire had done didn't amount to much in the end. And it was quite entertaining to imagine the great snob explaining to his wife how he had pinched the family savings with the help of a bent lawyer.

★

'Alexandra?'

'Yes.'

'Do you know someone called Carter?'

'Sounds vaguely familiar, yes.'

'The Curé's brother-in-law?'

'Ah, yes, of course.'

Alexandra considered her husband with some concern. At half-past twelve, he still seemed sober, and he appeared to be getting interested in perfectly uninteresting people. She had just bumped into him on her way out of the stable, where she had asked Albert to unsaddle her horse and lead him back to the paddock.

'Have you spoken to Carter about, er, about . . . '

'About what?'

'The past.'

Maybe he was drunk, after all.

'Could you be a bit more explicit, Michael?'

He looked at his feet and reddened slightly, then studied his fingernails. Finally, he muttered almost inaudibly:

'The IRA.'

She stared at him wordlessly, as if waiting for anger to reach the paroxysm stage before she gave him a slap.

'Michael?'

'Yes?'

'Never say those initials again, do you hear? Not to anyone – no one, no one at all.'

She felt only repetition would bring home the seriousness of the situation.

'I hope you haven't gone and done anything clever, telling it all to this, er, Skinner chap?'

'Carter,' Bollington corrected her.

'Yes, or to anyone else. You hear me?'

'Yes, Alexandra, but I just wanted to know whether you . . . whether you've told anyone.'

She frowned.

'I think you're going to have to explain a couple of things to me, Michael. Let's go in.'

'I might have a little whisky. It is apéritif time.'

'No.'

★

Sue Brimmington-Smythe was standing at the kitchen window, her head back, one hand on her hip and the other stroking her raven hair. She looked out at the rain and sighed, then, as if suddenly remembering a job to be finished, went over to where a fish-shaped corkscrew hung on the wall. She opened the fridge, hovered between two bottles of white wine, and finally chose the Sylvaner, having overdone the Bergerac the night before. She had sold the restaurant with art school at Saint-Jory which she had been running for ages, and could not wait for work to be finished on her new house so she could resume the hectic rounds of parties at which the English in the region all met, chattered, and got drunk. The sampling of guests was impressive. In the expatriate world of the Dordogne – permanent exiles, part-time ones or just occasional ones – Sue Brimmington-Smythe acted as a sort of *Burke's Peerage*, a living *Who's Who*. Less respectable than those august publications, but every lunch, every dinner, every evening was like a page read out of order, alphabetical or otherwise.

The building work, being done by Joshua, was sufficiently advanced to revive the festivities, but the pile of gravel in front of the barn, the caved-in roof of the sheep-byre, and the lack of tiles in the hall meant still not being able to invite certain friends or acquaintances whom one would have liked to see again.

She heard the sound of a motor, of tyres scrunching on the gravel that still covered only half the yard, followed by the inevitable slammed door heralding, as it were, the passage to another time, another world – that of the courtesy visit. For a few seconds everything hung suspended, waiting to see what kind of visit it would turn out to be – very friendly, very studied, boring as they come, or whatever.

'Ah, it's Richard Carter. He hasn't been round for ages. Do you know him?'

She was addressing Johnny McGuire, who was sitting at the kitchen table, his long legs crossed, his upper half leaning back slightly, drumming the fingers of his right hand on the arm of the rustic chair as he waited for the Sylvaner to be opened.

'Not very well. I've met him. Once or twice.'

Johnny McGuire bit his lower lip.

★

After his brother-in-law left, Carter had been assailed by an unpleasant thought. And yet so obvious. That only Sue Brimmington-Smythe could know so many people; and, consequently, it was entirely possible that she was the author of the pages that made fun of him with such impeccable cruelty. He knew she knew Bollington, even if she didn't like him; McGuire and his wife were friends of hers; and he, Carter, had managed to get himself invited to her little get-togethers and be charming. On the other hand, it was hard to tell if she knew the fair-haired fool who worked for Bollington and murdered scientists to save monkeys and weasels.

Yes, of course. Everyone knew everyone else. And, most of the time, had bugger all to say to them. So everyone made up all kinds of interesting stories about themselves – and at the end of the day you could never quite know who you were dealing with. And as you trotted out your own lies, as he had done himself so many times, you couldn't help wondering whether the person you were talking to wasn't doing exactly the same. All those ex-professors and former diplomats and cricketing heros arrived here, in the Dordogne, to a world where nothing was ever checked up on simply because no one could be bothered to do so. It wasn't worth it. Except, of course, for this writer. Who remained anonymous to them, relishing saying too much about them and not revealing why.

When the doctor arrived, a rakish French gentleman with a small grey moustache, Carter took the opportunity to slip away.

Stopping in the middle of the courtyard, he too admired the work in progress and wondered how much it could be costing. He also hoped it would not be wholly successful.

At the front door, Sue Brimmington-Smythe welcomed him warmly, though without allaying his suspicions. He tried a joke, but it fell flat. He went into the kitchen where he saw Johnny McGuire, who gave him a little wave. For perhaps a quarter of a second, Richard Carter thought he had fallen into a trap. He accepted a glass of wine mechanically, even though it was little early for him.

'You know Johnny McGuire?'

'Yes, yes, we, er . . . we've . . . er, met.'

They shook hands with a nod. McGuire . . . utterly incapable of doing anything without that detached sarcasm – disdain, one might almost say – you never knew where you were with him. But Carter still found him pleasant, or, more precisely, admired what he stood for, because he was perhaps one of the very few genuine members of this club. However, Carter's distrust was growing by the minute, if for no other reason than that he kept running into him, and always at a bad time.

They launched into the usual small-talk, in which they were all well versed. It could go on for weeks. As he held forth about a garden nursery where they sold foxgloves incredibly cheaply, Carter wondered if Sue Brimmington-Smythe and McGuire had been talking about the book, and therefore about him, before he arrived. Had she, if not written it, read it at least? After twenty minutes of this fruitless play-acting, Carter concluded that between the queen and the knight there was a sort of checkmate. The best would be to wait for McGuire to leave, provided he didn't stay too long, and have a word with him outside in the yard. For he felt that, of the ad hoc association between those the book incriminated the most, McGuire was not only the most genuine but also certainly the most trustworthy, to whom he would have to turn for protection against Bollington and his vegetarian. Especially Bollington, in fact, with his dangerous mix of shotguns and whisky. Mind you, the other guy used bombs . . . Sue Brimmington-Smythe interrupted this line of thought with a question about his wife.

'Still much the same,' responded Carter, with a shrug and a little sigh, as if to indicate that he too was suffering greatly. McGuire clearly had no intention of moving, and Carter realised he couldn't stay very much longer. McGuire was talking about his debts and the poverty he was living in while Sue laughed expansively, with that rich laugh of the well-brought-up English with which they convey, to each other, the illusion that no catastrophe could possibly be anything more than a huge joke. Carter decided to let them carry on in that vein and finish the Sylvaner between them.

★

'Listen, Michael,' said Alexandra Bollington.

A preamble he always found somewhat daunting. The last time she had started like that, it had been to persuade him to lend his yacht to the IRA. She had gone on to explain that in World War Two the IRA had been a German ally. He had liked that a lot because, like many Englishmen of his class, Lord Bollington had two fantasies – dressing in women's clothes, or in Nazi uniform. But he had a feeling that his wife's suggestions were going to have nothing to do with either of these.

'Are you listening, Michael?'

'Yes.'

'Right. You must get in touch with Carter and suggest you meet. As you already have.'

'Yes, Alexandra. Here?'

'Absolutely not. Tell him I don't know about it, that I've got guests, make something up. Or, no, I'll make it up for you.'

'But in fact you're just as incriminated as I am.'

The accuracy of his remark caught her by surprise. For a moment or two she was silent. She even wondered if she could really trust her husband. After considering, in record time, the various avenues open to her, she selected the best.

'Yes. But there's no mention of me in the book, just you. According to you, anyway. I really must read it.'

'Yes, Alexandra.'

'Get in touch with Carter, because he's certainly the quickest-witted of the lot. Are you with me?'

She gave him no time to think about this, or to wonder whether the quickest-witted wasn't in fact himself. He decided to trust her.

'And here is what you're going to say . . .'

3

'We're meeting at our friend Richard Carter's,' said Lord Bollington, 'to evaluate the risks to which we are exposed by this writer and what he says about us.'

Carter raised his head sharply. Who could have inspired Bollington to be so eloquent, so clear?

Turning his empty glass in his hand and staring down into it, Bollington made it clear he had no more whisky. Carter had got the message, but chose to make him wait rather than respond at once.

'It's only a book,' said McGuire, 'so let's not get carried away. Actually, I rather liked some bits.'

'The bits about yourself, perhaps?' asked Olson. 'Your wife like them too, did she?'

'No, the bits about you,' replied McGuire with a sideways grin.

'Gentlemen, gentlemen,' interposed Carter, obviously very annoyed: 'Mr Bollington is right.'

'*Lord* Bollington,' corrected the party concerned.

The other three turned to him as one and regarded him in silence. Clearing his throat, Bollington got up to fill his own glass:

'But I am *lord of the manor*,' he muttered, as the crystal decanter clinked against his glass.

'Can one really be incriminated by a work of fiction?' Olson wanted to know.

'I don't know,' replied Carter. 'The problem is there's no one I can ask.'

'You mean you haven't got a solicitor to take care of your affairs?' sneered Bollington.

Carter's face tensed.

'May I help myself?' asked McGuire.

Carter was at his wits' end. He was beginning to think he would get nowhere with this gang of blinkered snobs. They couldn't see that what was left of their lives, in this Dordogne to which they were all attached if only in the material sense, was becoming rapidly irretrievable with such published declarations. And there was promise of a sequel. His blood suddenly ran cold. He had just heard a creak from the ceiling. His wife was awake. With frantic gestures he told them all to be quiet. Not daring to utter a word, they watched their host as though he had gone out of his mind.

'Not a sound,' he said, making for the stairs with stooped shoulders.

Pointing to the ceiling, he tiptoed up the staircase. As they watched, the three shook their heads, raised their eyebrows and made a variety of grimaces to convey a mixture of understanding and concern.

He nudged open the bedroom door. It was dark.

'Marie, Marie,' he called.

The only reply was a slight moan, as though she were having a nightmare.

'Marie?'

The sound of a sheet, a rustle of sickness-impregnated linen, and he closed the door again like a mother checking that her child is asleep. Back down in the sitting-room, he motioned that everything was all right, and wondered whether McGuire, Olson and Bollington hadn't taken advantage of his absence to gang up on him.

'What are the real dangers?' he said, back in his armchair, to continue the discussion.

'Perhaps we ought to eliminate the danger before we evaluate its size. Otherwise it'll be too late.'

It was Olson who had spoken. McGuire said nothing. Carter began to change his mind about Olson. Could he have underestimated him?

'Can't we write to the publisher?' suggested Bollington. 'To get in touch with the author and find out his real name?'

At least, thought Carter, Bollington had realised the name was a pseudonym.

'True,' he said, at pains to treat Bollington with great patience, 'our first job must be to *identify* the author.'

'Well, there's no great difficulty there,' said McGuire offhandedly.

His words cast a chill.

'I beg your pardon?' said Olson, separating out his syllables so slowly as to be almost threatening.

McGuire was also contemplating the bottom of his empty glass. Now he brought his head up sharply and gave them all an ingenuous look, like a child who thinks he's been naughty.

Olson persisted:

'What exactly do you mean?'

McGuire shifted in his chair. Carter had never seen him so uncomfortable. Bollington was listening and watching closely, but with all the whisky he was finding it hard to remember Alexandra's instructions. One thing was sure: she had said Carter was the most intelligent of the four. So he looked at him and nodded. But just then Carter wasn't saying anything. He was looking at McGuire as if he were a fish out of water.

But Olson would not let go:

'No great difficulty identifying the author?'

McGuire shrugged, as if out of modesty.

'So who is it, then?'

43

'A retired copper.'

'In the Dordogne?'

'In the Dordogne.'

'Does he have a name?'

'Do we know where he lives?'

But, to Bollington's mounting exasperation, McGuire would only nod. At the same time, though, no one dared ask the real name of the cop McGuire thought he had indentified as the author. As if they were scared of reaching the answer too hastily, of having to take decisions, of moving on to the next phase of operations.

'Where does this information come from?' asked Carter with a frown that made him even uglier.

'I can't reveal my source.'

Sue Brimmington-Smythe, Carter immediately realised. It explained McGuire's being there during his own visit. And their way of changing the subject . . . unless, of course he had made up the story to cover Sue Brimmington-Smythe herself. Or himself. Or their complicity. Carter decided it was better to say nothing and leave the rest of the interrogation to Olson. Bollington's eyelids were getting heavy. Carter could not blame McGuire for covering for Sue Brimmington-Smythe. He rather liked her too. But the situation remained dangerous. He sat back and waited.

'The name Derek Spencer mean anything to you?' asked McGuire, turning deliberately to face Carter.

That changed everything. But Carter didn't even get time to think. He repeated the name softly, like an incantation, and then went shakily over to pour himself a whisky, moving like an alcoholic who has been dry for twenty-four hours.

Still wearing his sarcastic smile, McGuire nodded.

Bollington had sat up, and Olson looked from Carter to McGuire. He was waiting for an explanation.

'Spencer lives in the Dordogne?' asked Carter.

'Yes,' replied McGuire, as if he had just won at cards and was pocketing the money.

'Who is Spencer?' demanded Bollington.

Carter did not dare reply, because he would be obliged to go into the details of the poisoning he had committed twenty years previously, revealing to his companions the gravity of the situation in which the book placed him. But if Sue Brimmington-Smythe knew Spencer and had pointed him out to McGuire, then she too must know all. Spencer in the Dordogne: he couldn't believe it – and the deranged sadist now writing books!

For that, too, was the Dordogne. Coming to bury oneself here among the trees, off some winding road, always eventually running into someone from England, from the past. Actually it rather reminded him of Cambridge, where he had been a student. There, he was for ever running into some childhood friend who had not gone on to Eton with him, to remind him, like some sort of conscience of origins, that he came from the petty middle class and had ideas well above his station. How often had he heard, over a Dordogne dinner-table, that Mr So-and-So knew Mrs So-and-So, they had been neighbours in Yorkshire, Derbyshire, Kent . . . And if he asked whether they had moved here at the same time, together, the answer was always the same: No, they'd met again here purely by chance.

'If you don't mind, I think we're getting a bit ahead of ourselves.'

It was Olson who spoke. Carter felt immediately relieved at not having to expand on the relationship he had once been forced to maintain with Spencer. Hours and hours of questioning with the smooth hypocrite, followed by his shouting colleagues. It had felt like being trapped under a cathedral bell at midnight, the voices resounding like notes against the concrete walls of the police station. A place whose existence he would never have suspected. In his grey cement cell, he had often been reminded of the Spanish Inquisition. Similar thoughts struck him at lunch or dinner with his brother-in-law, who made a point of appearing in his cassock, even for family meals.

In his hellish side-chapel, Carter took to reciting a Latin prayer of his own: '*Habeas corpus, Habeas corpus.*' He knew for certain his guilt could never be proved in the poisoning of his victim, and he had clung to his faith so fervently that the case against him was eventually dropped. Despite the fact that, when he was being released, Spencer, smoother than ever, again told him he was convinced he was letting a murderer go free.

Carter turned to Olson, pretty sure he must be right. The man spoke with a common accent which he made no effort to hide.

'First he makes us read a book which talks about our, er . . .'

'. . . peccadillos?' The suggestion came from Carter.

Olson didn't know the word, but approved anyway:

'Then all of a sudden McGuire turns round and tells us he knows who wrote it. It's all too fast. And he won't even say where his information comes from. I find it all a bit odd, myself.'

Bollington was amused to see McGuire a bit put out and Carter somewhat thoughtful. His wife Alexandra hadn't thought events would take this turn.

'Do you think,' he asked, 'we'll have to kill Spencer?'

An icy silence followed this suggestion. No one could really tell if Bollington was joking again or if his question was at least partly serious.

'I'll not kill anyone,' said McGuire lightly.

Still rankling, Carter spoke up:

'No one said anything about killing anyone.'

'You,' said Olson, speaking directly to McGuire, 'will do like all of us. Whatever decision we come to, you'll be part of it. Get it?'

McGuire turned to Carter, but the latter would not meet his eye.

For a few moments a heavy silence hung over the group, and they could hear the upstairs floorboards creaking. McGuire had lost his amused, slightly arrogant look. Now he in turn got up, wordlessly, to pour himself a whisky.

'No one mentioned killing Spencer,' Carter repeated, almost with a twinge of regret in his voice.

Now, looking at each other, they felt like children who had gone too far in a grown-up game of terrifying, and now inevitable, consequences. Fear gave way to despondency. They all knew that each of them was feeling it would have been better if they had never met, never heard of the Dordogne. And for one brief, shared instant they all regretted that they had not just been ordinary little wage-earners, small shopkeepers in their nice little English country towns, where they could have led irreproachable lives – the daring glass of port on Sundays in front of the fire with the little dog at their feet, regular hours, and a loving wife, so they could have grown old peacefully, annual holiday after annual holiday, in some boring place or other.

But it was a bit late for any of that.

'I'd like to know how come our friend McGuire heard about this retired policeman.' Olson was returning to the charge, still talking as if McGuire wasn't there.

Still hesitant to say it came from Sue Brimmington-Smythe, Carter was wondering how long they would keep going round in circles:

'If McGuire can't say . . .' he began beseechingly, causing McGuire to look at him astonished, and Olson suspiciously. Carter added:

'Let's avoid any hasty decisions.'

It was Bollington who, to everyone's surprise, spoke next:

'If the author's a cop, then he may be trying to provoke us

by writing this nonsense. Perhaps he's waiting for us to show ourselves, to come down on us.'

There was, Carter thought privately, certainly some truth in this. Especially since Spencer had been so openly threatening at the end of the business. But why would he persecute the others?

'Even if, er, Spencer knows me,' he pondered aloud, 'why would he know all of us?'

'Because a cop, even a retired one, has access to all the files he wants to consult,' suggested Olson.

'There's no file on anything to do with me,' McGuire put in.

He regretted saying it at once, because he realised he was turning the other three against him.

'It was you,' responded Olson, 'who told us Spencer wrote the book.'

'Just a simple deduction, on the basis of information that . . . that someone gave me.'

'Who, for Christ's sake?' Olson cried.

'Not so loud, you'll wake my wife,' said Carter, tight-faced, adding in the same tone, 'Sue Brimmington-Smythe.'

McGuire shot him an accusing look. Carter shrugged.

'We had no choice.'

'She knows Spencer?' asked Bollington. 'He goes to Mass?'

'Pff, no. She just knows everyone.'

'And was it she who told you Spencer wrote the book?'

'No.'

'Has she read it?'

'I don't know. I think not.'

Carter was cross with himself for initiating the exchange between Olson and McGuire. It reminded him of times he had spent with the Spencer in question. But they had no choice.

'You think not?'

'You're beginning to get up my nose.'

'My wife, my wife,' muttered Carter hysterically.

'And how about if she wrote the book? You just said she knows everyone.'

'Well, she doesn't know you.'

The unspoken social comment escaped the notice of no one, and Bollington burst out laughing. Olson's annoyance was the more because he had to recognise it was accurate.

'Perhaps she got her information from Spencer and wrote it.'

It was a poor counter-attack, but perhaps worth trying.

'Where does this copper live?' asked Bollington.

'Near Saint-Saud,' replied McGuire, as if giving up.

They had now taken a big step forward. As no one had anything else to add, Olson decided to seek refuge once more in small-talk, to reassure himself and persuade his companions that things weren't necessarily that bad.

'When the Chinese commit a murder,' he explained with a distinctly unvegetarian smile, 'they all stick a knife into the victim. That way, no one can betray the others.'

'What's that got to do with it?' slurred Bollington.

'As we're all in the same shit,' replied Olson, 'we can all do like the Chinese.'

Bollington found the idea of being compared to a Chinaman absolutely irresistible. Bursting out laughing, he started going on about it. He realised the others were now fed up with his jokes, but he couldn't help it.

'I'd have thought,' he said, 'that as you're the one who's already comitted a homicide, you'd know the techniques, the, er . . . you know, and you could be the one to, er . . .'

'. . . put to death?' Carter finished. He thought it an excellent idea, even though he had put it somewhat strongly.

Olson had perhaps steered them back into jocular mood, but he thought this time they were carrying it much too far.

'Out of the question,' he said between gritted teeth.

It was becoming clear that beneath the jokey schoolboy atmosphere there lay a truth: these bastards were ready to gang up on him because they found him socially unacceptable; they would have liked to get him, the proletarian of the group, to carry the can.

'Out of the question,' he said again.

And he reflected that in any case these bourgeois types were not as distinguished as they would like it believed. The book that lumped them together demonstrated that perfectly.

'Coming back to more serious matters,' said Carter, who, no doubt because of his age, had taken on the role of professor, 'we've agreed that the danger must be removed. And we were, I feel, definitely on the right track. It seems to me clear that this character, this Spencer . . .'

How much longer, McGuire wondered as he raised his eyebrows, before Carter dropped this pompous tone? But although he noticed McGuire's face-pulling, Carter was not to be put off.

'This character deserves a lesson. We ought, all together . . .'

'Yes, give him a good scare,' concluded Olson. 'Shake him up a bit.'

'Nothing more,' said Carter reassuringly, turning to McGuire.

McGuire was now too tired to think. And decided that perhaps they were right after all.

'The matter of modality determined, it remains only to choose the moment.'

'What?' said Olson, in reply to Carter's suggestion.

'What he means,' explained McGuire, 'is, when are we going to beat up Spencer?' Having comforted himself with Carter's whisky, he was starting to speak more hesitantly and swallow half his words.

'But first, are we absolutely certain that it is this famous Spencer?'

'Besides, that is, what we know from Sue Tiddlington-Jones, brought to us by—'

'Sue Brimmington-Smythe,' amended McGuire.

'Her, yes. Otherwise, it could be someone else.'

For an instant, Carter thought of his brother-in-law. If proof were needed of his guilt, he would invent it, no great problem. He even permitted himself a fleeting smile and raised his eyes to the ceiling, above which his wife was carefully tending to her sickness, just as in the book they'd all been dismissing. Carter couldn't know it, but at that same instant Olson was thinking how funny it would be to tell these stupid fuckers that his own wife Oriel, or more precisely the exasperating Norma, had written the book. But he abandoned the idea rapidly, because he realised it was impossible.

It was then that Bollington declared:

'There's also a chance that the doctor . . . er, the doctor who looks after your wife, that is, Mr Carter, could be the guilty one.'

From the way they all looked at him with nasty, sly smiles, he saw they knew that the raffish old rake with the moustache had become his own wife Alexandra's lover. It was in the book. It had, for the moment, slipped his mind.

'No more whisky?' Bollington demanded, by way of distraction.

Carter fussed about a bit and then said he would need to disappear to the cellar for another bottle. He had the sneaking impression that they were again suspicious of him. Unaware of why, he told himself it was simply that kind of situation.

McGuire was sprawled in his armchair, gaping open-mouthed up at the ceiling, like someone asleep with their eyes open.

'Of course we'll have to meet again before fixing on any precise action,' Olson observed.

'Where?' asked Carter.

'Your place,' determined Bollington, mindful of Alexandra's words under all circumstances, especially after half a bottle of whisky, as though his wife was always the active part of his brain, the part alcohol could not reach.

'You look worried.'

'Be quiet.'

'Mark?'

'What? I've just told you to be quiet.'

He had left untouched the tofu which she had prepared, with little love. She was going to tell him she wanted a separation, that their planets were no longer fully compatible, that she thought perhaps the waves . . . but she had found him in a foul mood before even embarking on her little speech. He was fiddling about nervously with his fork, his face hidden behind the long fair hair which formed a curtain on each side. She didn't dare speak. It was he who broke the silence.

'Do you know someone called Sue Brimmington-Smythe?'

'By name. Why?'

'Ever met her?'

'I don't know.'

'Who did you hear about her from?'

She was tempted to respond to his questions with questions of her own, but felt this was not the moment.

'I don't really remember, I . . .'

'Make an effort.'

'I know I must have heard Alexandra Bollington mention her. The Bollingtons know her. Why don't you ask Alexandra?'

He raised his head sharply and looked at her as if seeing her for the first time. It was quite a good idea. All it would take would be to get in touch with the bitch without the husband's knowledge. Not too difficult. But – how could he drag her into this business without the slightest idea of what she knew and didn't know? Even that absolutely cretinous fucker Albert deserved better consideration than him. He got up smartly and decided to go for a little walk outside.

'Mark? There's something I wanted to say.'

'Not now.'

★

'Well?'

Alexandra Bollington was sitting in an armchair that was much too big for her. She had to reach out to use the arms at all, and her toes barely touched the floor. Wearing round-toed house-shoes and with her square-bobbed hair, she looked like a 1920's débutante. The floral pattern of the chair made a crown about her head, but her words and her tone were anything but ingenuous.

Seated on a Willam Morris chair that was far too small for him, Bollington gave his account of the evening at Carter's.

'Spencer?' she concluded.

Bollington shrugged. He could not believe that such a slip of a woman, this Irish girl from a farm where they dug peat, could terrorise him so. In fact he preferred not to think about it. He wanted a drink. He drank a pint of beer for breakfast every morning. Pale ale. A light beer to set him up. He knew perfectly well that alcohol weakened him – in the face of life, money, his wife. So what? At least he had the honesty to recognise that he liked being drunk.

'Do we know this Spencer?' he asked his wife.

'No.'

'Olson had doubts.'

'About what?'

'About Spencer being the author of the book.'

'But in any case, it was certainly Spencer who arrested Carter in England twenty years ago, there's no doubt about that.'

Bollington gave another shrug.

'Unless he's lying,' she added, as if talking to herself.

'Why should he lie?'

'I don't know.'

Set now on continuing her reflections alone, Alexandra Bollington's sharp little foosteps took her to the door, which she opened abruptly.

She gave a little cry, at which Bollington rose from his armchair. There he stood, open-mouthed and wide-eyed, paralytic with fear. Marmaduke. How long had he been at the door, eavesdropping? No way to tell. But judging from the position he was in, he had also been trying to peep through the keyhole. He couldn't have seen anything because of the little key that was always there. He was sweating and blushing, his wet lips trembling slightly. Not daring to look at his father, his first gesture was to fling himself upon his mother and press his cheek to her stomach. She stroked his hair mechanically, then turned to her husband as if to say 'I know what you're thinking, and I also know you'd like to give him a hiding, but I absolutely forbid it.' Bollington understood perfectly. And poured himself a drink to show he had surrendered, but that in exchange he was permitting himself what had been forbidden previously. The silent exchange occupied barely a quarter of a second.

Her voice soft, Alexandra Bollington turned back to Marmaduke:

'Come on, now, you know it's not nice to listen at doors. Go to your room.'

With a barely audible 'Yes' the boy used the back of his hand to wipe away a tear from the corner of his eye and gave a sniff. Then he moved away very slowly, with his usual flaccid, repulsive lethargy. It was perhaps what infuriated his father most. This manner of being, so namby-pamby, so viscous. Surely he had heard his mother's footsteps making for the door, had realised she would open it and he would be caught? But he hadn't even had the gumption to straighten up and at least pretend he just happened to be going past the door. It was this incompetence in deviousness that made him even more unbearable in his father's eyes. Although quite aware of this, Alexandra Bollington was assailed by doubt; she wondered if it wasn't, rather, some ultimate form of perversion. Pehaps Marmaduke had wanted to be caught spying on them, so as to force his mother to humili- ate his father by a show of authority. He had perhaps been hoping to see, or to feel, his mother's authoritative look forbid- ding Bollington any reaction.

The two had never forgiven Bollington for the name he had imposed on his son. Bollington himself found it rather a joke, having christened his son in the same spirit that had allowed him to call his dogs Hitler and Goebbels. And then, Marmaduke did after all have a certain ring to it, the kind of name a duke in 1856, or a general in 1902, might have given his son. Bollington thought they both distinctly lacked humour. Alexandra would have liked him to be called Hadrian or Sebastian, perhaps even Maximilian. But Marmaduke . . . He had not yet heard the end of it.

Whenever the boy was in a situation where no one knew him – itself a rare event – he would introduce himself as John, with anxious sidelong looks, for fear it might show on his face that his name was really the unthinkable Marmaduke.

Alexandra Bollington watched him with protective pride as he mounted the grand staircase and turned to give her a last, smiling look. And she was touched at the sight of his short, stubby fingers as they stroked the wide banister, it too of stone.

★

When he awoke, McGuire thought for one very brief moment, perhaps the time it took to take in the morning's real chill, that he had had a ridiculous dream in which he had been compelled to kill, or at least maim, someone he didn't know. Then he remembered having incriminated Sue Brimmington-Smythe in the eyes of dangerous men.

In his dressing-gown, he made himself a cup of tea and went out into the château courtyard. His feet were bare inside a pair of old Churches, now shapeless after years of lack of care.

He looked over towards the horses' paddock, as though he hoped he might find some solution there. Looking up, he saw a thin column of smoke coming out of the chimney. The fire he had lit the night before, still burning the huge oak logs he had piled on to give himself a semblance of comfort.

Fire . . . He could, for instance — to escape from the other three and the crime they were about to make him commit — set fire to the house and disappear. His wife would get the insurance, and he could let her know he was still alive and where to join him. It seemed crazy. But no more so than beating up an English copper retired in the Dordogne. Solution number two was to kill the other three. No, mathematically it didn't make sense. He could report them to the police, get them watched. But somehow that didn't fit with his code of honour. But he was beginning to wonder if the time hadn't come to dispense with it.

5

It was indeed Spencer, no doubt about it. Two hours spent waiting behind the steering-wheel of his car had given Carter the satisfaction of recognising his former torturer. Somewhat more stooped, a bit more hair gone from the temples. But it was him. Spencer. Come to live here, almost next door, not even bothering to conceal the fact. His name was in the phone book. Under Saint-Saud, in a little hamlet not far from the lake. At least it was clear where to put the body if he succumbed to a heart attack, for example. Carter gripped the wheel, as if it were Spencer's neck in his hands. His knuckles turned white. And the appearance of that silhouette at the door of the restored farmhouse (in lousy taste, moreover) removed the last of his doubts. Recalling the words he had exchanged with Bollington, McGuire and Olson, he thought of them with affection, like brothers almost. The three people left on whom he could count.

The grass in Spencer's garden was a deep green and cut short. Everything was maintained meticulously. Smelled of petit-bourgeois, thought Carter. Spencer had got into his car, an ultra-sober Rover, green, yet again. He appeared to have no dog. But that would have to be checked. Spencer got out of the car to shut the gate, then turned towards Carter's car parked a hundred metres away and screwed up his eyes. Carter switched on and reversed off at high speed. He must absolutely not mention this detail to the others. Impossible to tell if he'd been recognised, of course . . . but even so. If Spencer wrote such well-researched books, he must know Carter lived here and would be able to recognise him. He would just say that he'd gone to reconnoitre and had found Spencer in a relatively isolated restored farm cottage, probably an old cowshed. It probably used to be a sheep-barn. To reach his gate, you had to leave the road and take a dirt track for a hundred metres. There were only two windows in front, but Carter had no time to check the rest of the house. He was quite unable to shake off a certain fear: the man who lived here, even if now vulnerable, was the very same one who had inflicted on him, Carter, the most profound terror and appalling doubts, the man who had sought to destroy him and had almost succeeded.

★

Laura McGuire came into the kitchen in a whirlwind of kids. The barking of the dogs added to the din. She was used to it. But she pretended not to notice the greasy plates piled on the draining-board and, over there, the dried-up dog turds, to judge from their grey colour despite the general damp, must have been deposited beside the pine cupboard only a few days after she had left.

She had called the previous day to say she was getting home earlier than planned. When Johnny asked for an explanation, none was forthcoming. Two of his daughters, clinging to the legs of his once white but now dirty grey trousers, were holding up their faces to be kissed. The other, older children had gone over noisily to turn on the television and plonk themselves on the sofas which they shared with the dogs and cats.

It was grey and cold. The house's sombre interior seemed even damper than the landscape Laura McGuire had been driving through while her children squabbled in the back of the car. She spied, on the corner of the shelf, the postcard showing a sunny view of the proud English manor with its huge rooms which she had just come from. Then she raised her head to look Johnny McGuire in the eyes and give him a kiss on the lips.

'I hope you're not too cross with me,' he said, sweeping his arm to take in the kitchen: 'I've been, er . . . very busy.'

She raised her eyebrows and kept smiling, but this time with one corner of her mouth slightly lifted.

Without a word she kissed him once more. He felt his heart tighten, here in the bosom of his family, while his thoughts were on the times he had been spending with Carter, Bollington, and that other bloke, and the ludicrously infantile situation he had got himself into.

'I'd love a cup of tea,' she said. 'The road from Bordeaux was frightful. And the children have been quite ghastly.'

She sat down at the big pine table.

He should be asking her questions about her stay in England, for news of his mother-in-law, but he couldn't do it. The world surrounding himself and the future belonged entirely to the nightmare of the past few days, to the book . . . the book. He remembered now. It was on the bedside table. He had forgotten to put it away, and she was bound to be surprised to see he was discovering a taste for literature.

'You're very quiet. Not happy to see me?'

He produced the usual protestations, and then went over to the drinks cupboard for a fresh bottle of whisky.

'Whisky at this hour?' she asked, to the sound of the cracking of the metal cap as it was unscrewed.

Turning his back to her as he served himself generously, he was still wondering what he should say. He didn't even notice that she was saying nothing. She watched him, sitting on her chair, surrounded by bags, her old Barbour chucked across the table and still with that scent of elsewhere, of journey, of fatigue that hovers around the newly-arrived.

'What's going on, Johnny?'

'Huh?'

'You look worried. Something's happened while I've been away, something you're not telling me.'

She was already imagining some fresh financial disaster, a bit of the roof blown off, a car crash, a court order saying the house was to be seized. And she felt slightly guilty about spending these few days in the comfort, the luxury even, of England, leaving Johnny to deal with all their domestic problems on his own. Coming to sit next to her, he said things were all fine, took a nervous gulp of whisky, and finally managed to talk and smile more or less normally as the familiar family sounds once again filled these vast, cold rooms so recently draped in leaden silence. It was only now that he realised. While Laura and the children were away, he had suffered from that surrounding silence. Now it was something else: the silence over his past and future activities gnawing at him from inside, like some secret sickness.

★

Bollington was seated at the head of the polished mahogany dining-table, facing his wife Alexandra. As she took a mouthful of the extremely expensive red wine he had gone to buy in Brantôme, she looked him directly in the eyes. Challenging him. He knew very well about what. To mention, without shaking, the doctor's visit that afternoon. While he was in the gardens giving Marmaduke a shooting lesson, she had been in bed with her lover, the white-moustached old rake. In fact he was hard put to it to work out whether it was the doctor's white moustache or his wife's infidelity which disgusted him the more. He glanced at Marmaduke tucking into his wild boar stew, lips and cheeks smeared with gravy.

Two days earlier, Bollington had made Marmaduke finish off the wounded boar. While the huntsmen held it to the ground, he handed him a knife and told him he must plunge it into the heart to cut short the animal's suffering. Bollington looked on with a sarcastic smile as Marmaduke came forward shaking and breathless, his face a shade of green.

'Sharp, neat and clean! Sharp, neat and clean!' Bollington was shouting, his hands on his hips. There was blood everywhere.

It was obvious that Marmaduke was smearing the gravy everywhere in revenge, darting sly looks over his repellent hands. A disgusted Bollington had lost his appetite. He did not begin to realise how fascinated he was by his son's beady brown eyes observing him so furtively. He wondered yet again, and to no effect, just what went on in that head.

Alexandra was watching him, as if to say 'You just dare say something, you just dare tell him off!'

He thought back over her infidelities. He was dying to talk about it, but realised now was not the moment, he couldn't give them that pleasure. Especially not Marmaduke, now wiping himself on his already soiled white shirt.

'Delicious, this wine,' said Alexandra as she raised her glass to eye-level.

She allowed herself a slightly sardonic smile. Simply amazing, she thought, how this man, this wine-sodden brute who spent his whole life killing things, could sit transfixed before her, in his chair, not daring to broach the one subject he had on his mind at this precise instant. Her little romp with the doctor . . . Her smile vanished suddenly and she sat up.

'What is it?' asked Bollington.

'Nothing.'

She answered so sharply that he decided not to pursue it.

Michel . . . the doctor. Michel. Michel, her lover, who treated the McGuire children and told hilarious stories about the family. Michel, who treated Carter's wife. It remained to be seen whether he also knew Olson. But she had never spoken to Michel of her years as an active IRA militant. Anyway, Michel's English wasn't good enough for him to write a book. Though come to that, publishers always had at their disposal people who

61

could ghost-write. It would have been interesting to know if Michel also treated the cop. Spencer.

'Penny for your thoughts, Alexandra?'

'Oh, nothing,' she repeated distractedly, her eyes unfocussed, fork halfway from plate to mouth.

Bollington arched his eyebrows and reached for the carafe to pour himself another glass of wine. The effort made him short of breath.

'And yours?' she inquired, the sardonic smile back in place.

'Oh, nothing,' he muttered, gazing at the blood-red liquid that filled his chalice.

'You've been seeing him again, Marie. You should not. It is a sin.'

'Oh, please . . .'

He was a bit shocked by this answer. Coming from his sister, he had expected something somewhat more sugared.

'And Richard – he's never here, always up hill and down dale,' she added, as if just realising that she had spoken a trifle sharply.

'Does he not look after you properly?'

'Oh, yes, of course he does. But he flees from this sickroom atmosphere. Look at me,' she continued, lifting her hands a few centimetres from the sheet in sign of impotence.

Her brother thought that if she had the strength to keep up her liaison with her doctor, which she confessed to him as regular as clockwork every week, the sickroom atmosphere must surely get dissipated from time to time. He cleared his throat and joined his hands, as if for prayer. Except he wasn't praying.

'Does he go to church? To confession?'

'Who?'

'You know perfectly well, Pierre.'

'The doctor?'

'Michel, yes.'

'Of course not, Marie.'

'Could you not stay a little longer, Pierre? I'm bored.'

He had risen from his chair and was walking round and round. Occasionally his fingertips would brush something she had brought with her from the house where they had grown up together, currently serving to decorate this sickroom, this scene of adultery. To these souvenirs were added foreign objects in unusual colours which both intrigued and displeased him – a small Wedgwood pot of a nauseous blue, showing antique figurines, draped and in profile. It was hideous, and yet he could not tear his eyes away. Then there was the picture of the church with the square tower and the rolling, treeless countryside with the grazing sheep and, on a ridiculous little neo-Gothic shelf, cloth-bound books with English titles which he did not understand.

'Stay, Pierre, talk to me a bit,' she said, rousing him from the disagreeable reverie that had fastened on him.

She exaggerated her sick person's tone, which annoyed him. With a sigh, he sat back down on the straw-bottomed chair with the straight, hard back.

★

'Mark?'

'Yes?'

'There's no more money.'

'What do you mean?'

'In the bank, there's no more money.'

'And what do you expect me to do about it?'

But the correct question would have been 'How do you know?' For Oriel would have been hard put to it to reply that she had been to the Caisse d'Épargne in Thiviers to empty the account and get on the train back to England, when she had been told that because of the overdraft she could not withdraw even ten francs.

'Couldn't you ask Bollington for some? You've been working for him and he hasn't paid you. You're forever with him, you spend your life at his place. What are you doing?'

The alternative was to meet a man who would take her to England – or indeed anywhere, what about Spain, Florence, Venice, Acapulco, anywhere. But mind you, the chances of that happening here . . .

'I'm watching television.'

She couldn't deny it. For days he'd been doing nothing but. Or else vanishing altogether. She even suspected him of secretly spending the money he was making. But on what? Gambling? That wasn't like him. But then he hadn't been like himself recently – he'd been more like that absurd character in the thriller she had read. No doubt about it. And that made him a dangerous man. A murderer – and when she came to this conclusion, she couldn't understand what it was that was making her provoke him. Something stronger than her. She walked over to the television and switched it off. She had hardly begun to turn back to look at him when she felt a violent heat assault her right cheek as she toppled backwards. The ceiling whirled and the television crashed beside her. Only now did she feel the pain. Mouth wide open, she uttered a scream which quickly turned into a bellow of rage. She wondered breathlessly whether he was going to kick her where she lay. But he looked down at her for a few moments, arms akimbo, then turned away without a word and went out.

6

'You say the house is isolated?'

'Totally. But visible from the road.'

'I wish our friend Carter would consult us before going prowling around the presumed culprit's house,' observed Olson.

'Really? Perhaps you would tell me why?'

'Because obviously we must act together,' replied Olson.

'Not any more.'

At his words, they all turned towards McGuire, who had deliberately not touched a drop of alcohol since the meeting began, held as usual in Carter's sitting-room.

'And what does that mean, exactly?'

'That I'm pulling out.'

'Do you think this is a game of cards, McGuire?' asked Olson. 'You're "pulling out"?'

He put his arms in the air and waved his hands about like a pair of demented marionettes, repeating, 'He's pulling out, he's pulling out, he's pulling out,' his words accompanied by a sulky pout to ape McGuire's arrogance and express his own disbelief.

'It's definite,' cut in McGuire firmly, to put an end to the fooling about.

★

He had had the phone call from Carter the previous evening, summoning him to yet another meeting in the presence of the other two. Apparently they had been watching the house of this retired policeman whose name he, McGuire, had given them, and they intended to agree on a course of action this evening. On his way up to bed, he had decided he would not go all the way. By some sort of, oh, sense of honour perhaps, he would come to this meeting and tell them to their faces his reasons for pulling out. He had to speak to Laura first. She was still reading a story to the two youngest children. As he waited, he sat on the bed and unbuttoned his shirt without noticing the cold. Coming in a few moments later, she made for the bed and got under the duvet fully dressed. Only when she had warmed up did she change, by means of a series of contortions, into her pyjamas.

'Laura, I need to talk to you.'

'Now?'

'Yes, now.'

'Not something serious?'

'I don't know yet. It'll depend.'

'On what?'

'Actually, on you.'

She raised her eyebrows, then got up again and went to sit in the sagging old armchair. She crossed her arms and rubbed her shoulders, and declared:

'I'm listening, Johnny.'

'Right, then. I have a confession. You know I love you and that . . .'

He wasn't accustomed to this kind of declaration, and the new situation made him every bit as uneasy as what he had to confess.

'Don't tell me you've met some woman and want to take off with her?'

'Of course not,' he said as he raised his head. Almost tempted to laugh, he asked, 'Why do you say that?'

'I don't know, you start talking about confessing something, you say you love me and all that. Isn't that how adulterous confessions usually begin?'

'It's nothing like that. It's to do with money.'

'Nothing new, then.'

He tilted his head to one side, with a questioning look:

'You know the money that's been put in trust for you to have in four years' time and which allows us to just about survive here because when that day comes we'll be rich . . .'

'Hmm.'

'Well, a few years ago, I managed to get my hands on that money and made some lousy investments with the help of a crooked lawyer. Are you with me? The money is no longer there. We will never get out of this poverty. It's totally my fault. I robbed you and I lied to you, to you and to your family. So what happens next, now, is up to you.'

'That's it?'

'Isn't that enough?'

She shrugged her shoulders and looked at him tenderly.

'My poor Johnny, I've known for ages.'

'What?'

'The whole thing. I even talked to my mother about it again in England. And to her boyfriend. He was all for starting proceedings.'

'Against me?'

'Partly. And against the crooked lawyer, as you call him.'

'Got quite a nerve, I must say. He's only your mother's boyfriend, not as though he was part of the family . . .'

'In any case, I spoke up for you. Not very difficult, actually, as Mother helped.'

Johnny McGuire suddenly saw his mother-in-law in a new light.

'She defended me?'

'She did it for Daddy. It was Daddy who discovered you had got hold of the money Uncle Bertie left for me. He could have killed you. Only Williams, the crooked lawyer as you call him, was a cousin of Daddy's. And for the family's sake Daddy wanted everyone to keep their mouths shut about it.'

As she spoke, with the rather bored tone of someone who is repeating the same story for the tenth time, she was examining her nails and therefore did not see that her husband was watching her, dumbfounded. Torn between the comfort of knowing that the matter was ending fairly satisfactorily and the humiliation of having been the laughing-stock throughout, in every way and in everyone's eyes – his in-laws, his wife, the people he had invested with, and Williams – or, as he had just learned, cousin Williams.

★

'I'm not killing anyone,' McGuire repeated. 'It's not hard to understand. You've gone mad. You don't kill a guy because he's written a novel, even if what it says is true.'

'If you won't mind, er . . . Johnny,' suggested Carter with the air of the experienced man generously showing friendship to an idiot on whom he is about to lavish advice, 'you don't know the man in question. We know now that . . . I have had occasion to, er . . .'

'I'm not killing anyone.'

He hesitated to say that for him it had become in any case pointless, but thought that such a declaration could put him at risk. Even Carter had obviously gone over to the other side. For good. He could no longer be counted on.

'In any case,' Bollington chipped in, 'no one's mentioned killing. We just want to intimidate him.'

'Exactly!' exclaimed Carter, who knew perfectly well that nothing could ever intimidate Spencer. 'Exactly!' he repeated, 'we just want to teach him a lesson, shake him up a bit, make him want to drop it. To think this man has been watching us, prying into our private lives, using us with no good reason. The bastard, he . . . he . . .'

Carter was getting carried away. He had turned bright red, his jaw clenched. But a coughing fit prevented him from finishing.

'Johnny,' declared Olson in a cold, deep, metallic voice that was quite unlike him, 'you've got a family, children. They're back, if I understand correctly . . .'

'Who told you that?'

'Never you mind.'

'Who told you that, you bastard?' McGuire shouted, clenching his fists. 'In any case, you leave my family out of it,' he added, pointing at Olson. 'Otherwise, it's you I'll kill!'

'Gentlemen, gentlemen,' Carter interrupted: 'Let's be reasonable.'

'I will not be reasonable!' shouted Olson.

'Richard? What's going on? Is everything all right, Richard?'

'You've woken up my wife! Bloody idiots!' hissed Carter between clenched teeth. 'Nothing, darling,' he called up: 'Nothing. We're playing cards, and a couple of my friends are having an argument. You go to sleep now.'

'I'm sorry,' said McGuire, a little put out by the quavering voice that had come down from heaven.

'I'd better go and see,' Carter excused himself.

Without waiting for an answer, he went into his usual act, stooping slightly like a hunchback and going up the stairs on tiptoe although it was too late.

McGuire and Olson were avoiding each other's eyes. Johnny was making efforts not to drink, so as to remain calm and work out the best way of extricating himself from the situation. It was all too much. Bollington was frowning, wondering what Alexandra would have said, and feeling that things were going wrong in spite of everything. He did know one thing, though: they would have to rely on Olson. And it struck him as funny, to have to set store by this servant of his to get out of the shit. Not for a single moment did it occur to him that he had done little else throughout his entire life.

Carter finally came back down. Olson had not been idle, and had come to the conclusion that if he didn't corner McGuire this very evening, he would be exposing himself to a dangerous traitor. It would be possible to shoot him after Spencer, maybe even before. But it would be better to limit the damage, and to get McGuire through blackmail.

'It's for tonight,' he said.

'What's for tonight?'

'Spencer. We're going tonight.'

'Have you gone mad?' asked Bollington, while the others looked at Olson in bewilderment.

'We've, er . . . got nothing ready. An ex-cop . . . er . . . surely he's armed. We haven't made a plan.'

'We don't need a plan. We know where he lives. There are four of us. We knock on the door. We say we've broken down – a car-crash, someone's hurt, we need to phone.'

'Ah, I see, like that film on telly the other day,' put in Bollington. 'I saw it – it was great.'

'What if he saw it too?'

Olson shrugged.

'And if he's having people round?'

'At half-past-one in the morning, his friends will have gone. Talking of which, what time is it?'

No one dared answer. Olson turned to the absurd chiming clock on the wall.

'Quarter to midnight,' he announced, in case the others suddenly couldn't tell the time. 'We need thirty-five minutes to get there by car, going at a reasonable speed. Carter's told us the house is isolated.'

'And we kill him with, er, what?' chuckled Bollington.

'I've got a gun in the car,' said Olson in reply.

'What make?' Bollington showed sudden interest.

'Oh, just an old thing from Manufrance. Semi-automatic, four shots. Pellets or bullets, whatever you want.'

'Not bad.'

'It's not much, seeing that you never go anywhere without that elephant gun of yours. Get that in the face, and you can't even recognise the body. Have to identify him by his watch, but I'd planned to nick it.'

Bollington and Olson burst out laughing. For a moment, McGuire thought his lungs would burst. A feeling like a screw-driver gouging from left temple to right. He cast a glance towards Carter, eager, in the face of all logic, to find an ally. Carter was looking at his shoes and smiling. McGuire found it hard to believe he shared Olson's and Bollington's sense of humour. In actual fact, Carter was picturing Spencer, reduced to a splodge of blood and flesh, at his own front door with his roses and his little gravel path. It was this that had brought on the joyless smile. While McGuire could of course not be certain, it now came home to him that Carter must be lost to his cause. Three men gone crazy, like hunting dogs who have just scented the blood from the wounded animal. He had about half an hour to escape them, and already knew it was impossible. Since he had nothing more to lose and would wake up next morning a murderer in any case, he decided he could have a whisky on Carter.

Olson and Bollington were still discussing the technical aspects of the assault – wounding Spencer with a hunting knife, perhaps. They didn't have one on them, and there was no point asking Carter if he had such a thing.

Olson broke off to eye McGuire, who was going over to the bar and muttering to Carter:

'May I?'

'This is no time to get pissed. Just a drop, to give you courage when you need it, but no more, right?'

McGuire did not reply. He drained his glass and poured himself another.

'You heard what I said?'

'Get fucking stuffed!'

'Calm down, for Christ's sake!' said Carter. 'It's no time to start bitching, either.'

'How much time left?' asked Bollington, who was also starting to feel a bit nervous.

Olson looked back at the clock. McGuire looked at Olson. And Carter looked at his feet, at his hands, at his knees, leaning forward on the edge of his chair, his head filled with the numerous and varied deaths of the man who had transformed him into a blurred mass of fear, mistrust and anxiety, into some humiliated animal, the man who had maimed his pride, had made of him, when he thought about it clearly, a little old man before his time. He also blamed his wife for that, but that was another story. In any case Spencer could pay for her too. His smile broadened.

'I'll just, er, have a little whisky too,' said Bollington shyly, turning to Olson with a worried air.

Olson smiled at him with benevolence and patience. With a nod of his head, Bollington helped himself. No one spoke now. There were occasional creaks from overhead as Marie Carter stirred in her sleep. McGuire had reached the stage that follows anxiety, a sort of leaden resignation. It was no longer the prospect of beating up a man that weighed on him, but the prospect of being caught and tried for it one day. A still vague and indistinct prospect, however. The world ceased to exist beyond the confines of this over-decorated room; and time was now suspended, reduced to the twenty minutes between them and their departure. McGuire had told his wife he would be home late, that he was having a drink with some friends – it almost made him laugh, looking at the other three, to imagine referring to them as his friends.

Even Olson, trying to appear relaxed and continuing to behave like the lead dog in the pack, was starting to feel a certain impatience. He looked over at Carter, who seemed transfixed in an almost alarming immobility. McGuire was tracing the contours of his glass with his fingers, circle after circle. Enough to drive a man crazy. Four times in succession, Bollington raised his empty glass to his lips, to drain some long vanished last drop.

'Right, that's enough,' said Olson. 'We're off.'

Bollington and McGuire raised their heads without a word. Carter got up extremely slowly.

'But . . . what about the guests?' asked Bollington. 'It isn't even time yet.'

'What guests?'

'Spencer's guests.'

'We don't know that he's got guests. We'll see. If he has people, we'll come back later. We must move now, in any case.'

'Er, why?' McGuire gave a sardonic smile. 'You starting to crack? Afraid that any more waiting will make you give up?'

'I've just had an idea,' replied Olson, with a half-smile quite similiar to the one already on McGuire's face: 'It'll be you that knocks at Spencer's door to say you've crashed your car and you need to telephone. How about it? With your posh accent, he won't suspect a thing.'

'Sure,' replied McGuire, 'given your accent, I should have been suspicious a long time ago.'

Bollington burst out laughing, then immediately realised he'd made a mistake. But Olson just sighed, and reminded himself the time had come for action.

'Which car do we take?' asked Bollington.

'Did you come in the new LandRover?' asked Olson.

'Er . . . yes.'

'Then we'll take yours. Four guys in a big thing like that, looks a bit more normal than an ordinary car.'

'Ah, you reckon?'

'Yes.'

'Why?'

'Don't know, just like that. Like we're coming home from a hunting dinner.'

7

It certainly did feel like a movie. Bollington drove, McGuire in the front beside him. Perhaps because they still didn't trust him and wanted to keep an eye on him – Olson indeed taking the seat directly behind him. Carter was turned to the window, exuding an intensity and a concentration which had not been seen before. The white light of the headlights lent the night an oppressively soft quality. The new LandRover already stank of dog, of horse, of sweat, even dead game, blood of wild boar and deer. All these odours must have eaten their way into the seats and into the rugs that lay about in the back.

McGuire was thinking that he had never seen the man he was on his way to beat up. Come to that, neither had Olson. He didn't even know the sound of the man's voice. Perhaps, in the snatches of countryside revealed by the headlights, there lay an explanation for the acts which they had not yet committed but which had brought them together here on this road, at night. McGuire could still not really envisage the reality of blows, of blood, of the victim's screams of pain. For the first time in his life, McGuire caught himself philosophising. He wondered if his entire existence had not been in the image of this moment, a sequence of actions that were, more or less directly, decided for him – and which he obeyed, even when he had the illusion of being able to refuse. Acts that he was committing against his will and despite all logic, even when no longer necessary. He wondered if he were a coward. He looked at his companions.

Bollington was a dangerous idiot – was that a form of courage? Perhaps. Olson was a brutish bastard – and there again lay an answer to his question, no doubt. As for Carter, with his fixed gaze, tight jaw, motionless – he was still silent. He had lost his old man's look, his air of puny querulousness. There was a time when one thought his wife's condition might be rubbing off on him, but he was evidently rejuvenated now. His face was looking dry, his ugliness had turned terrifying, and his wild white hair made him look like a tired torturer. McGuire wondered whether, at the end of the day, Carter wasn't perhaps the craziest of them all.

He recognised the occasional detail, a gateway here, the corner of a house there, a turning, a tree that had been a landmark in the past without his even realising. He had the impression that the very purpose of this trip had caused the landscape to explode in a tumult of now insignificant details, lost in a white light that connected them to another, lifeless world.

'The headlights.'

All at once the darkness was total. Bollington had switched off the engine and the LandRover freewheeled into the drive leading to Spencer's house.

Bollington's gun was hidden under one of those large tartan woollen blankets that you spread out on the grass at a picnic.

'McGuire . . .' muttered Olson.

Without a sound, as though he had been a member of the Long Range Desert Group, Johnny McGuire opened his door, got out, and felt the yielding earth under his feet.

He saw the square red glow of a curtain in a lit window. He gradually approached the light, guessing at rather than seeing the front door next to it. Must listen before knocking. The outlines of the house became clearer with every step. Same for the garden, neatly tended. One could imagine the effort Spencer put into it every day.

McGuire crouched to approach the window. The grass lay

thick and lush, like a mattress. Slowly he straightened up, and made out the dark silhouette of a man at a table. There was a fire burning and a little jazz coming from a somewhat dated stereo.

There was still a chance to shout, to warn this man, lost in his comfort and his solitude, even to join him and withstand a siege by the other three, call the police, put themselves under their protection.

The man was leaning forward slightly. McGuire could hear a plastic clicking. The man was sitting upright at the table. McGuire realised Spencer was using a typewriter, an old-fashioned electric one.

Suddenly McGuire felt a decided distaste for this man, revealing everybody's secrets here from the depths of his home. A sneak. An informer. A man he had never met, who was willing to break up his marriage, his family, for the pleasure of sitting here like a rat in his hole, telling stories and making money out of the lives and deaths of other people. The cosiness of the room moved him not one bit. He felt something he would never have suspected – a sudden sympathy for Carter, Olson and Bollington. Having less to lose, he still did not share their anger. But as he watched the frenetic activity of this unknown man, he thought that if he got himself beaten up by the other three for revealing their darkest secrets, he would be getting only his just desserts.

He banged on the door.

★

'You seem a bit nervous.'

'It's nothing. I'm just, er . . . a bit tired.'

Naked to the waist, Michel Beynac was sitting in a chintz armchair in the middle of Alexandra Bollington's bedroom.

She was standing, looking through the window at the

night, repeating to herself her final advice to her husband before he left. First, don't be the only one to strike. Or the one to strike the fatal blow. Make sure McGuire doesn't leave alone. They must all four stay together, and come back without separating. She had not been reassured by what he had told her of McGuire. As for Carter, no knowing where one was with him.

'What are you thinking?' asked Beynac.

'Oh, nothing . . .'

For a long while, two or three seconds at least, she searched for something to say. Finding nothing, she added, mechanically:

'About our relationship, er . . . I love you.'

A little flat, but it would give her a couple of minutes' peace to think. It was then that she remembered that her lover also treated Carter's wife.

'You treat a Frenchwoman married to an Englishman, I believe,' she said, no hint of romance left in her voice.

'Why do you ask?'

'I met Carter at some dinner, and wondered if you knew him, what sort of man he is.'

'An uninteresting little old man,' replied Beynac with a shrug, aware that such a question, out of the blue like that, was not at all usual.

'What's his wife's problem?'

'Being married to him, no doubt. She's a great hypochondriac.'

'Really? So why continue to treat her?'

'Because she calls and that's how I earn my living. But I don't see . . .'

'It doesn't matter.'

Turning gently towards him, it was her turn to announce, smiling ironically:

'You seem a bit nervous.'

★

Spencer took the first shot full in the face. His body was thrown backwards, giving Bollington, Olson and Carter room to plunge into the house. He was already unrecognisable. Bollington emptied the second barrel into his chest. There was blood everywhere and pieces of flesh scattered all over the room. Over in the corner, McGuire was vomiting.

They felt they had produced an appalling noise, as if the boom of the two detonations continued back and forth from wall to wall, like the sound of the sea on some unseen beach. Their footsteps were heavy, pausing here and there to decipher the man's life from the details of this interior. The walls held framed illustrations, torn no doubt from Victorian encyclopædias, of birds, plants and butterflies, mostly in watercolours, all carefully aligned with the wallpaper. Books, of course, on pine bookshelves, and some rare editions in an antique bookcase. A single large armchair in front of the still-burning fireplace. Spencer was perhaps a widower. But there were no photographs of children or a deceased wife on the desk at which he had been sitting just a few minutes earlier, enjoying all this comfort and solitude. The knicknacks on one of the shelves included an affectedly overdone hand-painted scale model of an English cottage.

They looked at the ceiling, on which the fireplace cast shadows between the beams. They dared not speak, their voices feeling hoarser than usual. They resembled particles of violence in a healthy body. When their eyes met, they experienced a feeling of power mixed with fear and disbelief at the sight of the body, its head half torn off by the lead, sprawled grotesquely on a reddish Persian carpet now being made even redder with blood.

'The petrol!' cried Olson.

Bollington went out to fetch the fuel can which had stayed by the door.

Carter, recovered, was for a moment afraid Bollington might make off in the LandRover. But thirty seconds later, he was sprinkling the old floorboards.

'We're leaving traces everywhere, it's insane,' said McGuire. Having had time to adjust to the horror, he had recovered some semblance of common sense.

'Stop whining, you're a plague!' retorted Olson.

All the more so because McGuire was right.

'That's why we're setting fire to the house,' Carter explained, now completely reassured by the sight of Spencer dead and disfigured.

'If you really think that'll be enough, with the things the police can do these days.'

Shrugging, he walked over to the table where Spencer had been working at his typewriter.

Olson joined him, to look disdainfully over his shoulder:

'Hey! – he was writing poems, the bloody idiot!'

8

He had got home, perfectly sober, at half-past-two in the morning. Oriel was lying in bed, the Indian blanket over her, eyes wide open in the dark, imagining the outlines of the objects in this room which she had come to loathe.

He hadn't come straight upstairs to bed – she didn't understand. He had gone into the bathroom and turned on the tap – she could tell from the whistling sound in the pipes – and a few seconds later had gone back into the kitchen where he had put some logs in the wood stove, and had then come upstairs perfectly steadily, without knocking into the furniture or upsetting crystal pyramids and incense burners.

He slept until eleven o'clock the next morning.

★

'Where were you?'

'With friends.'

'It's not like you.'

'I just wanted to see people, get out a bit. How're you feeling?'

'Weak.'

Of course, that was all she ever said, like some crummy actress, a slight quaver to her voice. Weak. Like a sheep's last bleat on its way to the abattoir.

'What time is it?' she asked.

'I don't know.'

It was precisely two-thirty-three in the morning. He could tell by the luminous roman numerals on the alarm on the bedside table.

'Well, I hope at least you've had a nice evening with your friends,' she said, smoothing the sheet with the flat of her hand and tilting her head a bit to one side.

'A very good evening, an excellent evening,' he replied forcefully, almost shouting: 'A long time since I've had such an evening,' he added, with a smile which alarmed her. Then he stood up and marched out of the room, leaving her dumbfounded.

★

They had to leave all together in the LandRover and pick up their own cars to go home in. Three engines starting up. No one really wanted to hang around at Carter's for a final drink. The return journey happened in silence. A few kilometres away, they saw the flames rising behind the trees, carrying off Spencer's body, Spencer's poems, Spencer's novels. The gas heater blew up and woke the neighbours. The fire brigade took ages to arrive. The youngest fireman passed out when they found the victim's remains scattered about by the explosion. That had been Olson's doing – a speciality of his.

★

The house was asleep. But McGuire was finding it hard to get to sleep, despite getting drunk in the kitchen and inebriatedly feeling that he had come to a new lucidity. With the first few glasses, at least. He knew that when Olson and Bollington exchanged pleasantries – mainly in order to put him off, to frighten him, and indeed successfully – they believed everything they said. Their laughs, their rather brutish big boy manners, served merely to keep their real intentions half hidden. And he, McGuire, hadn't been the least surprised to hear Bollington's footsteps running at his back, followed by the explosion in his ears which had deafened him for long minutes. And all that vomiting he had done at Spencer's house – he was angry for making such a spectacle of himself. Even angrier for having pretended to go along with their game for so long. And even more so for having gone all the way. And now he was angry with Carter too, for having been the one to seek him out in the first place.

He had drunk three-quarters of the bottle and was hastening to fetch another while he could still stand, because he knew what was left wouldn't be enough. He smoked one cigarette after another, and ran through the scene as a series of exploded images that would follow no chronological order. The face, above all, of which nothing remained, just a huge red hole and a few strips of flesh around it like a ripped curtain. He expelled the smoke without exhaling, just opening his mouth so his head was engulfed in a cloud that would blur the images. His thoughts again turned to himself. And since he had drunk one bottle and opened another at once, he wondered whether he too was a hypocrite. He had always known Bollington or Olson would kill this man. Was it perhaps because he was afraid of them that he had let himself be dragged into it too? Or was it something worse?

He couldn't have said what time he went up to bed, nor what prompted him to abandon his chair and climb the stairs as if his body, freed of his spirit by the wine and by his guilt, was moving in some mechanical obedience.

When his wife smelled his breath next morning, she asked him nothing about his activities the previous evening.

9

Spring had returned. And in the months that had elapsed since that night of fire and blood, things had been amazingly quiet. The fine weather had come sooner than expected. Olson had got used to Oriel's long absences – he now called her 'the fat bitch Norma'. For some time she had been going to stay with a girlfriend with similar tastes and who wore long skirts. That was what she said, anyway. Only once did Olson wonder if she had found herself a lover, but when all was said and done he couldn't have cared less.

Carter, who was taking his wife's illness better, did not hesitate to be away for long periods. He took to sitting at the café in Thiviers with a glass of Suze, to philosophise on life and death in general. Spencer was dead, each sip reassured him. And what was more, it was he who had killed him. Helped, of course, by that bunch of nincompoops. But no one could take that away from him. He had dreamed of it during all those hours of interrogation. At every question, at every shout, every time the door opened and the man appeared with his amused smile, Carter had envisioned the worst tortures for him. He had wanted to outlive this man. It was unthinkable, unacceptable, that illness or accident should carry him off before he saw the end of Spencer. And the Dordogne had made it all possible – this wonderful land, with its countryside, its greenery, its marvellous food – it had enabled him to fulfil all his dreams. Almost all of them, anyway. When he thought of his wife, his face darkened momentarily and he called for another Suze.

Bollington was walking with a firmer step since living the adventure, and thought he detected in his wife's eyes (he still introduced her to all and sundry as 'Lady Bollington') a new touch of respect. In which, incidentally, he couldn't have been more mistaken. But he had nonetheless come to regard Albert with a certain disdain, as though this rubicund character no longer scared him. Why, imagined he, I'm capable of committing crimes you couldn't even guess at, you mere killer of pigs.

Only McGuire was still having trouble sleeping. He was now even poorer, and had sold furniture that had been his father's. He had even considered selling a horse, but changed his mind when he realised the dealer in question would have taken it straight to the slaughterhouse. And, particularly at night, he had strange dreams which he could not manage to fathom. In them, the details of that murderous night unravelled like a bottle of wine sent crashing to the floor, painting, in red, ridiculous scenes where he found himself surrounded by those men. Each time he thought of it, the more he detested them: he had become their accomplice.

PART TWO

10

It was of course Carter who first perceived the disaster. Six months later. Early October, to be precise.

He was carrying a shopping-bag in each hand that day, string bags which underlined his age and gave him a slightly absurd, womanly look. He walked along with complete disregard for the impression he was making in the streets of Thiviers. In a dream. He had lately taken to dreaming. That he was poisoning his wife. Every bit as successfully as he had slaughtered Spencer – because, even though Bollington had been the one to fire the shot, with time and impunity Carter had managed to convince himself that the real murderer had been himself. But in this episode of his murderous career, an imaginary one this time, he was acting alone. He pictured her at the instant of dying, eyes stretched in a final spasm, foam at her lips, raising a wasted arm and realising, at the very moment at which she gave up her soul, that she had been poisoned by her husband, Richard Carter. Her just desserts. In other versions, the agony was longer-drawn-out and he took the time to explain why he hated her so much, exactly how he had administered the poison – and if while he was doing his shopping there was a queue at the dairy shop, for example, he saw himself also telling her that it would soon be the turn of her brother, the priest, to go the same way. He was following the hearse, above all suspicion, when his happy dream was rudely shattered by the appearance of the dis-aster he had been least expecting: there, in the bookshop

89

window, a book bearing the same pen-name as the one that had led them all to murder. The same six letters to make the same English name, another ridiculous title. He shut his eyes for a few moments. Slightly distracted by a pain in his arm and realising the bags were the cause, he set them down, before looking again, open-mouthed and staring, like some psychopath or mental retard who can't figure out why the person he has just stabbed is dying. He looked round at the other books in the window. Then back to the first. He felt a migraine coming on. He felt a sudden urge for alcohol, a beer – a beer, yes, like the cure for a hangover the morning after. Looking up again, he saw the bookseller in his grey shopcoat, up on his stepladder arranging the God knew what on his shelves. He felt a wave of hate for the man, as though he were the author of the book. He felt somehow that he couldn't stay at the window for ever. But he was also sure he wouldn't buy this book from this shop. Although why not, seeing he was there anyway? As he approached the door and pushed it open, he realised he had left his shopping bags on the pavement. Turning back, he smiled drily at an old lady watching him, and went inside.

Without a good morning, he pointed at the window and said, 'The book,' as though the bookseller would understand at once. When the man raised his eyebrows, Carter again pointed at the book he wanted to buy, unable to say the author's name, the title already forgotten.

The shopkeeper nodded and said it had just come out, as he made for a table that held a score or so of copies. Carter didn't even dare take it when it was held out to him, as if afraid to burn himself.

'Er, would you have a bag?' he asked, without noticing the shopkeeper had already wrapped it.

Muttering excuses, Carter saw over his shoulder that there were two other customers waiting. His voice seemed to him far-off, carried on some dizzying echo. Nodding his head like an animal, he left.

As he got home, he spied the doctor just going in. A detail struck him, but in his bewildered state of mind he couldn't say exactly what. But the unease he felt at the incongruity of what he saw got mixed up with what he felt about the book, in its white paper bag jammed under his arm like an abscess. He decided he didn't care to meet the doctor, nor to enquire after his wife's health of this crook who was raking it in from the raving hypochondria in which she wallowed.

He went to the café, ordered the beer he had been needing and sat down in the back, breathing the smell of pastis which often reminded him that he lived in France. The book sat in front of him, in its bag. He dared not even take it out, but had to drink the beer and call for another before summoning up the courage to glance at the cover. The title was set against a bloodstain, with what looked like a Dordogne farmhouse and the shadowy faces of four men grouped in the background. It all seemed to him very distasteful. He began to draw some of the conclusions forced upon him by this object, sitting between him and his empty glass. First, in killing Spencer they had got the wrong victim. Unless the first book had been written by two people. Or someone else had written the sequel using the same pen-name. If, of course, it was a sequel. One thing was certain – this book had to be read, a prospect that filled him with horror. Not to mention tedium. And then, the others must be told. He was aghast at the thought of having to renew contact with his companions in misfortune. That hateful hippy, the pretentious, brutish Bollington, and McGuire . . . He had seen McGuire once since. At Sue Brimmington-Smythe's. At one of her soirées. After exchanging a few vague niceties they had decided to ignore each other. He had met Johnny's wife on that same occasion. A rather attractive woman, actually. After that, he had decided not to reply to Sue Brimmington-Smythe's invitations, preferring not to run into McGuire again. Why did the memory of the man's wife make him think of the doctor going into his own house to examine his wife? The second time this week. Because they had talked about him, that evening at Sue Brimmington-Smythe's. Because she knew him, he looked after their children. And he remembered what was unusual in the doctor's appearing at his door. No one had opened the door to him, and Carter always locked it when he went out. The maid was not there. So the doctor had his own key. That was a bit much. Unbelievable, in fact. His eyes fell again to the cover. Opening the book at random, he tried to recognise himself in one of the characters – and succeeded rather rapidly. He had been given the same name as in book one. Bollington's appeared a little further down, saying a couple of pretty stupid things which he found rather amusing. Casting his eyes to the heavens, Carter stroked his chin and wondered if this new publication meant having to murder some other author besides Spencer. The very idea weighed heavily upon him. Murdering writers could become as everyday as doing the washing-up, a tedious task to be accomplished with detestable companions. The third beer washed away his fear and his consternation, to leave only weighty despair. In this new torpor, his thoughts returned to the doctor. He stood up, put some money on the table, and left, eager to be home before Beynac had gone.

Too late: the doctor had left before Carter got there, lugging his shopping and his new book.

★

'Michael!'

Bollington started at the tone of his wife's voice. It was a long time since he had seen her so agitated.

'We were wrong, Michael.'

'What about?' asked Bollington absently.

Alexandra gritted her teeth, shook her head from side to side like a pureblood coming into a straight, and clenched her fists into her husband's face as he sat in his armchair looking at photographs of dogs in a magazine.

'About that copper. The one we killed. It wasn't him.'

'Don't understand.'

'There's another book. By the same author. It wasn't Spencer. Quick, call Carter! No! Hang on! Think!'

For, indeed, Bollington was not thinking. Try as he might, he didn't quite know what he was supposed to think about. Watching his wife, he could tell by her wrinkled brow that she was thinking, hard. Finally, she sat on the edge of a chair. Her fists still clenched, she moved her lips as though talking to herself.

'Have you read it, this second book?' asked Bollington, finally grasping the import of what his wife had told him.

Raising her head, as if she had momentarily forgotten he was there, she replied, 'Of course,' with an air of amazement at such stupidity.

'So what's it about, this book?'

'It says how you, Carter, McGuire and Olson all killed Spencer, presuming he had written a book that incriminated you.'

11

'The doctor's got a key to the front door?'

'Is that such a surprise?'

The energy and vehemence of her reply took him aback. Carter had expected his wife to start fretting the minute he came into the room. Noting his discomfiture, she decided to pursue her counter-attack with gentleness.

'Darling,' she began, reaching out her hand with a sad smile. 'What is it that worries you? You're often out when he comes,' – almost always, thought Carter – 'and you know I am rather ill,' she added with a sigh. 'I need to call him sometimes. I had a dizzy turn this morning. When you're not here, nor the cleaning-woman, I'm not sure about going downstairs. But you shouldn't be so worried,' she continued as though he had gone senile, 'I trust Michel completely, you know.'

'And what has he prescribed for you?'

He could see himself trotting off to the chemist's, to return with kilos of medicines costing the earth.

'It's over there,' she replied, indicating yet another of the all-too-familiar prescription forms.

Leaving him no time to reply, she continued:

'Bought a book, Richard?'

He looked down at his right hand, which still held the white paper bag. In his anger, he had put down the shopping in the hall and gone upstairs with the book still jammed under his arm, transferring it mechanically to his hand on entering the room.

'Uh? Oh, er, yes. Just a, er, distraction.'

'What is it?'

'Nothing, nothing interesting.'

'Can you show me, Richard?'

'You wouldn't like it.'

'How do you know? Show me.'

Again the weak smile. How easily, he thought, could he have smothered her with the pillow.

'Oh, just a thriller. To while away the time.'

She tilted her head and frowned, to show surprise. Carter used the silence to ask:

'Your brother coming to visit this afternoon?'

'No, why? He doesn't come every day.'

She had fallen for it, and he had managed to change the subject. She would have appeared crazy or suspicious, to keep insisting on seeing a book which, she had been told, was of no importance. He could see she realised this. Wonderful, really, how every time her brother the Curé's name came up there was either a respite or a chance to make her angry. Meanwhile, she continued to wonder why he was refusing to show her the book or to talk about it.

In a couple of determined steps towards the bedside table, he grabbed the prescription and stated:

'I'll go and get you this right away.' And after a sly silence, he added: 'And if you had a funny turn, best be careful.'

She opened her mouth to protest, but he had already closed the bedroom door behind him and was going down the stairs.

★

'Tell me again exactly what was said those two evenings you met at Carter's.'

Bollington furrowed his brow.

'It's rather difficult, Alexandra. We said lots of things.'

'Yes, Michael,' she said, again as though he were four years old, and indeed he was starting to annoy her.

'The chap you killed was, if I understand correctly, the cop who arrested Carter in England ten years ago. And, we gather, our friend had a little adventure of this kind, from what it says in the book. Am I wrong?'

'No, Alexandra.'

'Right. Now, would it be possible that this old ratbag Carter used the story simply to get rid of a copper who was still after him? Who first identified Spencer as the author of the book?'

'McGuire.'

'What?'

'It was McGuire.'

'And how did he know Spencer?'

'Through Sue Brimmington-Smythe.'

'I don't get it.'

Bollington of course hadn't got any of it from the start. He refrained from comment.

'Michael, I want you to read this book and tell me if what it says about how the murder took place is accurate.'

★

As he closed the book, Carter wondered why McGuire – or more exactly his character – was the only one in the second book not to take an active part in the murder. What was more, his literary counterpart acted with more courage than he had in fact shown. Of all the little band, it was McGuire who emerged the best from the fictionalisation he had just finished. Spencer's name had become Spender, which he thought showed a total lack of imagination on the author's part. But meanwhile, one thing was certain: they had got the wrong victim. And something else was more than likely: there was, as they said in the murder stories that had so delighted his childhood, 'a traitor in their midst'. Which created an additional problem, an immediate one. Who to telephone to fix a meeting? Who to discuss this new development with? Bollington? Certainly not. Unless the phoney lord were not the idiot he was taken for. Not very likely, but worth bearing in mind. Olson was both violent and hypocritical, a dangerous combination. He also had courage, although the second book did not spare him, describing even his defects rather exaggeratedly. Perhaps a way of covering himself if he was indeed the author, on the grounds that he would never paint himself as he really was?

★

'Alexandra?'

'Yes?'

'Should we call the others?'

'Not yet. You're not to do anything. Look after Marmaduke. From now on, I'm the one who's handling this.'

She got up and went over to the main stairs, where she shouted, 'Marmaduke! Marmaduke!' No answer.

'Michael, go and fetch Albert and, er . . . do something with Marmaduke, some shooting practice for instance.'

Bollington complied but, on his way out into the gardens, turned back towards her and considered her with a look that surprised her. After all, the evening of the murder he had told her everything and she had told him everything he had to do, all of it. Her social origins were very humble. And he had money. Was she devising one of those complicated plans which were quite beyond him, in order to get rid of him? She certainly had lovers; he knew it, everyone knew it, and he considered her perhaps perverse enough to have mentioned it in the first book in order to humiliate him yet further. Mind you, she was the one who had dragged him into that Irish nationalist business. And when he thought about it, he told himself he had been dead wrong, because quite frankly he didn't give a toss for the Irish.

The grotesque form of Albert had appeared at the front entrance to the manor, waiting for the orders about to be given.

'Albert,' Alexandra Bollington commanded, 'saddle my horse. If you will. I need to go for a ride to have a think.'

Albert went off with a grunt, watched by his masters.

'Alexandra?' said Bollington.

'Yes?'

'About your lovers.'

'Oh, not now, Michael, really not. We've already had this conversation, so let's not have it again.'

He watched her walk over to the stables, a few paces behind Albert. He wondered for a moment if she had slept with this gorilla of a man. He was not jealous, belonged in fact to the civilised class, but nonetheless thought that would have been a bit much – if only for the position it would put him in with regard to the servants. In fact, he could quite understand how a woman like Alexandra might be sexually attracted to an animal such as the hulking Albert. He himself had had a certain feeling for women who were screamingly vulgar and ugly. She had asked him to take care of Marmaduke. Not for the moment. He had work to do. He was sick of leaving everything to this woman now coming back towards him, booted, riding-crop in hand, on an immense thoroughbred, trotting determinedly to the woodland edge in the orange October light. It sometimes reminded him of the English countryside he ought never to have left.

★

'It's been six months since you last worked for Bollington. What's going on?'

Typical. Six months ago she wouldn't stop nagging him because he worked for Bollington, that he was, as she put it, his 'domestic'. And now . . .

'Oriel, I've never liked the man, you know that. I preferred to, er . . . break the negative relationship,' came the smooth reply.

'We've no more money.'

'What about your yoga classes at Champagnac?'

'As if that were enough. I'm fed up with yoga, anyway.'

'With yoga?'

'Yoga and all that rubbish.'

'I don't get you.'

'I'd like to know why you don't go back to Bollington.'

'I've just told you.'

'And how are we going to live?'

He leapt up. An instant later she felt a vast hotness on her right cheek, followed by a resounding pain. As she staggered back, her calf knocked against the coffee table and she fell onto the Afghan rug. She saw him above her, glassy-eyed, no doubt waiting for her to get up to hit her again. Without really knowing why and with no time to think about it, she shook her head frantically from side to side. Was she looking for an escape, a weapon? Before she could even answer her own questions, she received a kick in the ribs which made her double over. Then she heard a noise. The sound of blows, except this time she felt no pain. There was knocking at the door. Olson spun round, stayed stock-still for a second or two, pointed at her face, and said:

'You keep your mouth shut, you. Get it?'

He went to the door as she sobbed into the Indian cushions. It was Bollington.

★

'Mr Carter?'

He knew who she was immediately, and his first reaction was fear. It was Alexandra Bollington. He realised at once why she had come. He had finished reading the second volume of his own adventures the previous evening.

'This way,' he said by way of greeting.

He led her into the room he called his study, where the only work he did consisted of rehashing his memories. For a while now, his bitterness had overtaken his self-satisfaction. A sagging armchair presided, in the centre of a worn carpet in front of the small marble fireplace. There was a dirty glass at the foot of the chair, and school photographs added to the atmosphere of ageing masculinity. Alexandra Bollington realised that entering this room meant being allowed to spy on Carter's secrets, and that by the end of the interview they would know if they were allies working together, or enemies. For the moment, Carter was somewhat put out to see that Bollington's wife was taking matters in hand. She was obviously the man's brains. Yesterday, in fact, he had wondered if Bollington didn't fake stupidity to hide his real intentions. He could now answer these questions with a few adjustments: the brain that lurked behind Bollington's dimness was hers. A few moments of observing her, and he saw that. She followed him into the study with none of the stupid, pointless chatter, thus distinguishing herself from most English people around.

'Have a seat,' he said, indicating the armchair.

Sitting in the swivel office chair, he crossed his hands on his knees, leaned forward slightly, and started to sway from side to side in the most annoying manner possible.

'Mr Carter, I've come to see you on behalf, so to speak, of my husband.'

'I see.'

He now realised he had not even offered her a drink. Then, reflecting that 'Lady' Bollington was no more than him, just a simple bog-Irish girl and a murderer to boot, he lit up a cigar and said: 'You don't mind if I smoke.' It was not so much a question, more an affirmation.

'It wasn't Spencer,' she blurted out.

It was so sudden it almost made him jump. But having been on his guard from the moment she arrived, he contented himself with raising his eyebrows and, after a silence, answering a dry, barely audible, 'No.' Her eyes turned to the desk to indicate the book that lay there. He gave a nod. He did not really dare to speak, nor she to go too fast. She wondered if he might not have a pistol or a dagger in this ageing-bachelor room with its closed-in cigar smell, the hussar engravings hanging crooked against the dark green wall fabric. With a sigh, Carter gave the bridge of his nose a pinch. Alexandra Bollington cleared her throat and took the plunge:

'The description of the evening upon which, er . . . is it an accurate description?'

'Not entirely.'

'Of course not.'

'What do you mean?'

'That the person who wrote this book would obviously put a few discrepancies into the story to create a doubt.'

'Doubt?'

He knew perfectly well what doubt, having followed the same line of thought. But he simply wanted to see whether she had drawn the same conclusions, and whether her thinking matched his own.

'We quite simply can no longer be sure the author is not one of you four – yourself, McGuire, Olson, or my husband.'

'Or you,' replied Carter. 'There would appear to be five of us now.'

She could not suppress a smile. And in that instant, he found her attractive. He wondered if she had noticed, because she was leaning back in the armchair with her legs crossed, revealing a slightly bony but quite acceptable knee. Imagining her, among other things, as the mistress of his wife's doctor, he decided that women had simply deplorable tastes, although he nonetheless understood the allure the ridiculous old rake could have for these females. He searched for a word to describe her: she was not voluptuous, even though she tried to seem so; she was, he thought, 'spicy', and let it go at that. He had a fleeting vision of himself working together with her, two partners capable of killing or swindling anyone, any time, and making off with anything within their reach. With each passing scene of this furtive tableau, he felt himself grow more youthful. Meanwhile she had married a rich man, so better forget the dream, stop looking at her knee, and pay attention.

'It was in your interest that Spencer disappear,' she stated, comfirming his last thought, before she added: 'You've already killed a man in the past, if I've read between the lines correctly.'

'You refer to the first volume in the series.'

'Quite.'

Still the same smile.

'Do you really imagine that to get rid of some retired cop I would get into all this dangerous, pointless skulduggery? Oh, and I didn't know about your involvement with the IRA.'

He was right. Twice. But better not to admit it.

'Someone could have told you,' she said.

She saw she had been wrong to suggest it.

'Oh really, who? If we find who could have done that, we'll be getting close to the shit-stirrer that's writing these little novels. The only thing that escapes me, to tell the truth, is his motive.'

'Money, maybe?'

'That's not enough.'

'To get rid of you?'

Frank, if nothing else.

'Yes, and of your husband, and the other two. If I, too, have read correctly, and not between the lines, you had good reason to be rid of your husband.'

She raised her eyebrows, this time in real surprise.

'What reason?'

'Your lover.'

This time, she burst out laughing:

'Oh that! Michael couldn't give a damn.'

How utterly middle class of him, she thought, and continued:

'Anyway, I no longer have a lover.'

Could this be deliberate provocation, he wondered? As casually as he could, he ran his hand through his greying hair.

'How about if it was your lover wanting to do away with your husband?'

'But why would he want to do away with you?'

That brought him up short, smothering another dream before it had even begun. Nonetheless she chose this moment to conclude:

'I think it would be in both our interests to work together, Mr Carter.'

And her smile allowed the dream to take up where it had left off.

★

Bollington exploded with laughter at the state the Olsons were in, and for a while forgot the reason for his visit.

'A little lovers' tiff,' he commented. 'It'll sort itself out.'

But seeing his audience was not amused, he cleared his throat and turned to Olson:

'I have to talk to you, it's important. Come right away.'

Olson followed him to the car without a backward look. Not a little annoyed, he asked:

'What's happened now? I don't work for . . . '

'There's a second book.'

'A what?'

'A second book, same author. About us. About the murder.'

Bollington started the car without having to endure the protesting Olson, slumped in his seat looking straight ahead through the windscreen at this countryside he could no longer bear, in constant accusation, dragging up his past, chaining him to idiots like the one sitting next to him now.

★

Oriel sat on the bed and looked at the room. The Indian fabrics, the coloured crystals next to other mystic baubles, the furniture ludicrously arranged as a result of some feng-shui course – and all those utterly inane books which, over the last five years, had provided her with a stupid jargon that allowed her to fill the blanks in the conversation while she slowly died of boredom to the scent of joss-sticks, in the company of this vegetarian who had made her stop smoking and forced on her his simple life and his 'values'. In spite of all that, he was the slave of the ghastly Bollington, with his lurid jokes at her expense at which Mark chuckled obsequiously. A weakling, in a word, who had ended up frightening her. She put her head in her hands and started to sob.

Then, after several minutes of crying over her lot, she stood, straight upright, and went over to the mirror. Her cheek had started to swell up and take on a blueish tinge. Her gaze wandered over her violet shirt and wide, flowered dress. She loosened her clothes and let them fall to her feet. Though now totally naked, she barely felt the cold. Seizing the rustic straw-seated chair at the little desk, she started to smash everything in sight, sending knicknacks and bits of glass flying through the good and the bad vibes.

★

'I've read the book,' said Bollington. 'And, er . . . Alexandra knows nothing.'

Olson raised his head and wondered why Bollington would lie.

'The book claims that McGuire didn't take part in the killing. Or, more precisely, that if he was present, he was still against the idea of murder.'

'So?'

'So I've concluded that it was him.'

'Him what?'

'The author.'

'Before the first murder, I always said things were moving too quickly. That we should have thought.'

Thought. That seemed to be all anyone could say.

'McGuire would hardly have written a first book explaining how he swindled his wife.'

'Perhaps she's forgiven him. Or perhaps it wasn't true.'

Olson hadn't thought of that. He knew the crime he himself was accused of was genuine, that Bollington had indeed had links with the IRA and been involved in arms deals. And the contained fury with which the old man had contributed to Spencer's demise added weight to his sincerity. But there was nothing to tell them that McGuire's crime – of, incidentally, no importance other than purely domestic – was not in fact a pure . . . a pure fiction.

'Then how come McGuire knew about what involved us?'

'Through Spencer. Whom he then had shot by ourselves. It was him, after all, who told us he was the guilty party.'

Olson turned in astonishment to look at Bollington as he drove with a slight smile, looking straight ahead. He was thinking: Astounds you, huh? You stupid bastard. You wait, I'm not through surprising you, you'll see.

'So what are we going to do?' he asked.

Ah – finally! – he was being asked what was to be done. And none too soon.

'We'll shoot him.'

Olson sighed:

'Let's think.' This was getting crazy: 'Because,' Olson went on, 'I don't understand his motive.'

'What do you mean?'

'Why would he play that game?'

'What the fuck do we care about why?'

'What if there were two authors?'

'Two authors?'

'One for the first book – Spencer let's say – and a second who uses the same name and writes the second book to fuck with us. At the end of the day, he's not sure that Spencer was innocent. Spencer was on Carter's case, he could have had access to our IRA files and, er . . . the other things.'

'Quite.'

'As for McGuire, he could have learned from . . . what's that woman's name again?'

'Which woman?'

'McGuire's friend.'

'Er . . . Sue Brimmington-Smythe?'

'There you are.'

'She's also a friend of ours,' replied Bollington. 'More or less. Alexandra sometimes runs into her at Mass.'

'Is she Catholic?'

'Yes.'

'So the IRA stuff and . . . '

'Nothing to do with it.'

'You sure?'

'Absolutely certain.'

'What makes you so sure?'

'I've told you, it's got nothing to do with it.'

Olson thought he would check for himself, while Bollington was kicking himself for bringing it up.

'That still doesn't explain why he would do it.'

'He needs money. He could easily write the sequel and send it to the publisher in Spencer's place — tell the story with the same characters, getting himself half off the hook, as well as an advance that would solve his problems.'

'Bit risky. Anyway, as I understand it, he never opens a book.'

'Then his wife.'

Olson couldn't help being slightly amused to hear such an explanation coming from Bollington.

'Oh, *cherchez la femme*, you mean!' And he burst out laughing.

'What's so funny?'

★

The *femme* in question was busy washing up, surrounded by screaming, squabbling children. She was thinking how nice it would be to have an opening over the sink to look out at the countryside while she washed the chipped cups and plates. Johnny had gone out, and she knew neither where he was nor what he was doing. For a while now she had noticed that he was moving, almost seamlessly, from periods of euphoria to long moments of silence. He was drinking more, and it was starting to show in his jowls. After dinner one evening at Sue Brimmington-Smythe's, she had mentioned the death of an Englishman she had met, a retired policeman who had died when his house caught fire, and Johnny had spoken not another word for the rest of the evening. He had staggered back out to the car, and gone into hysterical laughter on the way home. Although already dead drunk, when they got there he went off to open another bottle of wine. When it was time to check that the children were asleep, he went into heart-rending sobs in their room – really embarrassing, and she had to pull him out by the sleeve before he woke them up.

When he was out, like today, she would lose herself in household chores – of which, what with the children and their poverty, there were plenty – so as not to think about the disasters awaiting him. Particularly on the road, coming out of a café.

She had been alone in the kitchen for five minutes, mechanically scrubbing at the large cups and their indelible tea-stains. The kids were upstairs or in the garden. And even though this momentary calm gave her time to worry and brood on Johnny and his transformation, it was still a respite of a sort.

When she heard footsteps outside, she couldn't help turning with a smile, like a B-movie heroine. It was not him. She saw instead a fair-haired man, rather tall, whom she couldn't quite place. He was sizing her up with a smile. She didn't know what to make of his expression. Was he admiring her shapeliness? Was he intimidated? Or in some way threatening? He still did not say hello. Narrowing her eyes, she carried on slowly wiping the cup in her hand. It was she who spoke first. In English, because it seemed clear to her that he could not be anything other than English – although she also realised, almost instinctively, that they were not of the same world.

His only reply was to ask:

'Your husband's not here?'

She concluded that he was distinctly threatening.

'Er . . . no, Johnny is . . .'

She had barely three seconds to produce a lie, and obviously it wasn't enough.

'Johnny's out,' she said, then added, 'but he'll be back any moment,' although she had absolutely no idea.

It was a way of letting this man in the creased, collarless Indian shirt know that he had better not try anything.

'Can I wait for him?'

She had not expected that. And before she had time to reply, he had sat down at the table.

'What do you want to see Johnny about?' she asked.

Quite possibly her husband had borrowed money from this man, who was now here to be repaid by force. What if Johnny did not return?

'Oh, it's er . . . I don't know . . .'

He chose to remain silent, looking from side to side. She was now sure it was something to do with money. As he had seemed embarrassed, she summoned up the courage to ask his name. With a start, he realised he had not introduced himself.

'I'm sorry. Olson. Mark Olson.'

She frowned. The name rang a bell. Then she smiled as it finally came back to her:

Oriel's husband?'

Oriel: she found it almost impossible to say the absurd name, but because these two hippies insisted on her being called that . . . As far as one knew, perhaps he insisted on being called Jupiter. She didn't give a toss, but she was still wondering what he was doing here.

'Oh, you know my wife?'

He seemed extremely surprised.

'Yes, er . . . we meet at Helen Rover's. You know, the painting group. Thursdays.'

McGuire had not told him their wives were acquainted. But then he might not know.

'Would you like a drink?'

They were getting back onto safe ground. To keep it that way, he asked for tea rather than beer or a glass of wine. And anyway, judging from the state of the kitchen, he strongly doubted there was either.

'Do you often see Norma?'

'Who?'

'Oriel, I mean.'

So her real name was Norma. What a joke, hardly surprising at all.

'Every Thursday.'

'Oh?'

Could it mean something? Was this female, right here in front of him, in fact the author and trying to cover for her husband? No, that was ridiculous. And McGuire still not back yet.

'Looks like Johnny's been held up,' she hinted heavily when Olson had drunk his tea.

'You don't know where I might contact him? It is rather urgent. Rather important.'

'Nothing serious, I hope.'

'Er . . . no. But pressing.'

'Would you like me to ask him to contact you when he comes in?'

In other words, a 'Piss off' which didn't leave him much choice.

'Yes, but do ask him to make it quick. Please.'

These last words, spoken with such urgency, made her realise that it was perhaps not a money matter, but something much more serious.

★

The day before he had done his best to show Bollington that they could not be sure McGuire was the culprit. The only reaction he got was a grunted, 'Yes, but still . . . ' It was if he had some other reason for wanting to shoot McGuire apart from the book and the poison-pen writer. And Bollington now seemed increasingly sure of himself – not necessarily a good sign. Personally, he couldn't care less whether McGuire got himself shot by the idiot. But the problem was Bollington would be caught if he acted alone, no doubt about that, and was liable to tell the police what had been going on. Bollington had given the impression that he was prepared to wait, but Olson did not always trust him. Alexandra Bollington had disappeared. He realised it would have been better to warn her. And now he found that McGuire's wife and Oriel knew each other. He tried to reach some conclusion from this unthinkable situation, but could not. He thought back to Laura McGuire. How could she have learned that he had planted the bomb that killed Dr Gordon? From the Bollingtons. They had known each other, because that was partly how Bollington had swindled McGuire. But would the Bollingtons have told their new 'friends' about their former IRA undertakings? Unlikely. But allowing for . . . How could she have known Carter's story? Through Sue Brimmington–Smythe, who knew Spencer. Unless McGuire himself knew Spencer, and had given Sue Brimmington–Smythe's name as his source to set them on the wrong track. And if he had known Spencer, it could explain his attitude that evening. All that weeping and vomiting – pathetic. It would also explain why he wasn't depicted as a murderer in the second book, and . . . that would mean the idiot Bollington was right. Astounding. And then, of course, in that case, everything personal about McGuire in the first book would be false, right down to the money stolen from his wife. He would have liked to meet this Sue Brimmington-Smythe, who kept coming back like an echo, and ask her, for example, exactly what kind of relationship she had had with Spencer. Because they only had McGuire's word for it. Though not really . . . it was Carter who had spoken the name, and McGuire had not objected. Perhaps that was wrong. Perhaps they were in it together.

★

'Richard?'
'Yes, Marie?'
'Come and talk to me.'

He sighed as he went upstairs. The door squeaked when he pushed it ajar. There she was, amid the pillows, with her yellow face and blue rings under her eyes. Pretending to be ill, shut up within these four walls, had finally made her look the part. She gave a pitiful sigh, although it aroused not the slightest pity in him.

'Did you have a visit, Richard?'

'Just the wife of an acquaintance. An Englishwoman who . . .'

'Oh, you English, always in one another's pockets. Like a club. You don't have your friends round in the evenings like you used to. Why not, Richard? It's a pity, I thought it was good for you to see people. It gave you a bit of a change from my company, which I know isn't much fun.'

Indeed, he thought, although he didn't say it.

'Who's the lady?' she asked.

'Lady Bollington,' he answered smugly, even though he knew there was no reason. 'Lord Bollington's wife. He was one of the ones who came round to, er . . . play cards.'

'Oh, yes, I've heard about him from my brother.'

'From your brother?'

'Yes. They're devout Catholics, you see, Richard. Lord and Lady Bollington go to Mass every Sunday.'

The tone in which she said these words. All that respect. If only she knew, poor dear. He felt like laughing out loud.

'You don't mind me asking about your friends, Richard? I wouldn't want you to think me nosy.'

'Tell me something, Marie. There's something I've always wanted to ask you.'

She raised her eyebrows. Waiting.

'With the Catholics, er . . . '

'Yes, Richard?'

'When you confess your, er . . .'

'Sins?'

'Yes, that's it. When you confess your sins, do you tell absolutely everything?'

'Richard, what a strange question!'

'Yes, I know, it is a bit — how can I put it? — . . . but you see, since I've met er . . . Lord and Lady Bollington, I've got very interested in these things.'

'Do you still see them?'

'On and off. As you saw, she came to see me yesterday, so . . . But could you answer my question?'

'I'm surprised, Richard. When we got married, you weren't in the least bit interested. I remember, you used to launch into such diatribes . . .'

'Never mind that. I'm interested now.'

'How odd.'

He clenched his jaw, burning to yell, Answer the question, or I'll kill you!

'Yes, right. So?'

'Richard, how could I answer you? Not everyone is necessarily honest. Sometimes people are afraid to confess certain shameful things to a priest, I don't know . . .'

'You, then? When you confess to your brother.'

'Technically, we can't say it's to my brother that I . . .'

'Fine — but do you tell him everything?'

'Come on, Richard!' She had found the strength to raise her voice. 'You know perfectly well I can't answer.'

The idea had come to him in a flash. Was Bollington capable of confessing his crimes, and those of the others while he was at it, to his brother-in-law? It sent a shiver down his spine. Because if that was the case, then the list of people he needed to eliminate was growing. It was unending.

'But a priest doesn't have the right to pass on to other people the confessions of his, er . . .'

'Of course not, Richard. Didn't you know that?'

The bottom line of the brief interview was nothing less than that, unbelievable though it might seem, he would have to check with Alexandra Bollington.

★

The immediately recognisable sound of the car meant Johnny returning. The engine . . . which she heard every day, a sort of leitmotif that summed up her world, a daily symphony which, with its major keys and its minors, its sharp notes and its flats, supplied the soundtrack to their days, responded to by the children's cries and tears, and the barking of the dogs. A world of noises that repeated themselves until sleep quietened everyone, and all the countryside with them.

Laura McGuire was upstairs, putting the children to bed. She looked at her watch, although she knew what time it was from having looked, barely ten minutes ago, at the kitchen clock, which she didn't like and wanted to replace.

She was going from the youngest children's room to that of the older ones, when she heard Johnny's step in the hall downstairs.

'Johnny?'

'Yes?'

A voice rendered shaky by alcohol. But never mind. He was in the kitchen, pouring himself a drink and calling up to her:

'Laura? Have you told anyone here in the Dordogne about the business with the money?'

'It's not important.'

'Perhaps, but I'd just like you to tell me . . .'

She sighed. She knew exactly what awaited her. Another drunken evening in which he would ask for the forgiveness she had already accorded him. He would wallow in self-recriminations. Tell her that if he'd known . . . that he'd thought he was acting for the best . . . that he would never do such a thing again . . . and she would have to refrain from telling him that since all the money was gone there was little chance of his doing so.

What she did not know was that he had come back from Périgueux, where he had seen, in a bookshop window, a second book by the author he thought he had killed, which he had bought and read in a café in the Cours Montaigne. He hadn't liked the part about him doing so much weeping. As he read he had got drunk on Suze. Why Suze? He couldn't have said.

'Hang on, I'm washing my hands and I'll be down,' she called from the small bathroom upstairs.

'Well, have you told anyone?'

Unbelievable.

'Oh, Johnny! Yes, just one person. So what about it?'

'Who?'

'Hang on, I'm coming.'

She soaped her hands as she had never done before. She was dreading this moment. The consternation, the anger, and all the rest. He would say that people talk in this place because they've got nothing else to do, and it was true. That he would be afraid to show his face, he couldn't stand people knowing his secrets without his knowing whether they did or not, it was humiliating. And he would not be entirely wrong.

She heard footsteps on the pathway outside. The stones crackled under large soles. He had gone out into the yard to wait.

'Coming!' she cried again, with a quick wipe of the towel.

But the only reply was a terrible crash. Like a thunderclap only drier, shorter, unusual. Then someone running off, a racing sound. All the noises, another music followed by silence, heightening further a small voice that called from one of the bedrooms – 'Mummy! Mummy!' – in answer to the worried voice of Laura McGuire as she called out:

'Johnny! Johnny!'

Johnny was dead, crumpled beside the sink, in the inevitable pool of blood.

12

'I'ld like to go to Mass.'

'What?'

'You're a Catholic, I believe. I would like to go to Mass. And ask you a few questions.'

'You've found faith?'

'Just a few questions because yes, I do have doubts, and I'm looking for some answers. I thought I might find them in the Church, you see.'

Alexandra Bollington couldn't suppress a smile. Nothing amused her more than seeing hypocrisy in action, her own included. And in her opinion Carter was giving a particularly good demonstration – and wasn't fooling himself, either.

★

'Oriel! Oriel!'

Wonderful, the way she was never there when he came back. One good thing, at least. Bollington, however, continued to worry him. Since the night they had killed Spencer, he had no longer been the same man. Olson felt he was coming to the end of a slow process of development. Bollington had become a killer. He had enjoyed the evening six months ago. And now McGuire absolutely must be told. Because Olson had seen that Bollington was indeed veering into the madness that had

117

stalked him from the day his parents dropped him off at the door of his Sussex prep school.

McGuire had not called. He wondered if his wife had passed on the message. And he dared not return to the scene. Maddeningly, the phone wouldn't answer. But anyway, he imagined he still had plenty of time. The same thoughts kept recurring, totting it all up. He didn't care if McGuire got shot, but it was so obvious Bollington would muff things, and then they would have to deal with the gendarmes. That must be avoided, and McGuire must be warned.

Meanwhile, he had decided to pay a visit to this Brimmington-Smythe who kept cropping up in conversation, and who knew everyone except him.

She was in tears at her kitchen table, on which there stood a half-empty bottle of red wine. At first, Olson thought she was dead drunk. Ten o'clock in the morning. A bit early, but not unknown among her compatriots in the Dordogne. What with the wine and the tears, he saw it would be better to postpone their conversation.

He had gone into the hall, approached the kitchen door hesitantly, and found her there. She had not yet heard him. He hung back a moment, wondering if he ought to clear his throat, somehow reveal his presence. Still time to retrace his steps; what he saw did not match what he had heard about this woman. Suddenly she raised her head and stifled a cry as she caught sight of him. She had been afraid, and her fear communicated itself to him through the look that passed between them. He had felt it intuitively the moment he saw her. Something terrible had happened. A presentiment, a shadow at the back of his mind or a barely perceptible shudder in the pit of his stomach. He wondered if these tears were not the logical consequence of the chain of events that had begun six months ago and to which he had contributed, even if she didn't know it. And now, this woman was looking at him as if he were a killer who had broken into her kitchen – confirming his intuition.

'Forgive me,' he said.

The two words served to re-establish some semblance of normality between them. A half-second of politeness that enabled him to continue:

'My name is Olson. I see I'm intruding. I'll leave.'

Wiping her eyes, she looked at the bottle and the empty glass beside it on the table. She instinctively wanted to make a good impression on this unknown man, rather than let him think he was dealing with an alcoholic who got drunk all on her own at ten in the morning.

'Forgive me,' she said in her turn. 'I'm not very well. I've learned of the death of a friend. Quite awful. Yesterday evening. Murdered. A gunshot. Maybe you would have known him, he lived locally – Johnny McGuire.'

★

Carter was now convinced that the key to the business lay in Mass. He consequently found out about services, without a word to his wife. He was hoping in this way to surprise his brother-in-law – catch him coming out of the confessional, for instance, something like that – he still didn't have any very clear idea. Only, he would have to go alone. Alexandra Bollington had told him she always had masses said in the private chapel at the manor, that as much as possible she avoided mingling with the ordinary faithful. The idea displeased Carter, who had last attended a religious service at least forty years earlier – no, more – in the Church of England chapel at his public school. He was sure that with the Catholics it would be somehow different. Far more complicated, even though he knew, from having vaguely read in the papers somewhere, that things had changed a bit. Perhaps he wouldn't be noticed in the crowd; he would limit himself to moving his lips, head lowered, as if inspired, and he would stand up and sit down slightly later than the congregation. It could always be put down to rheumatism.

He needed the time and place of Mass. But he wanted to make no mention of it to his wife. Nor did he want his brother-in-law to be warned, or to notice him. He would have to get to the church in advance and hide behind a pillar. Churches always had pillars in them.

'Going out!' he called up through the ceiling for his wife's benefit. She didn't answer. He hesitated a few moments. Should he go up and explain he had to go out, almost as if asking for permission? Or show his maturity, his virility even, and grab his coat and go off to the café like other men? He finally opted for the latter course, although he still felt a lump in the pit of his stomach as if he were playing truant. The church was locked and, unlike the cinema, there was no timetable on the door. He decided a café would be the best place.

He chose one that was more traditional than the others, with wooden tables. Without being able to say why, he had the feeling that the idea of Mass went better with a rustic décor than with pinball machines and a lottery terminal. Wandering about Thiviers, he found an establishment that about corresponded to what he was looking for. But when he asked, in his somewhat stumbling French, when the next Mass would be held, they laughed in his face because the owner was a radical socialist who detested priests. The clients started exchanging wisecracks. One chubby fellow seated in front of his glass of beer, bawled out:

'I saw the Curé the other day, and he said to me, "Why don't you come to Mass? Are you worried the roof fall might come down about your head?" You bet I am, I replied!'

Another man took over, making a mock sign of the cross:

'I told the Curé, "I make this one work −" placing three fingers at his forehead − "to feed this one −" the fingers now down at his stomach – "without making these two work at all!" ' – placing his fingers on one shoulder and then the other. It was a joke they had all heard a hundred times before, but they burst into laughter. Carter responded with a stiff little smile and a few nods. He ordered a glass of white wine and drank it in little gulps, standing at the bar, his back to the room. He could still hear bursts of talk, but couldn't tell if they were making fun of him or had moved on to something else. He stood hunched over, his eyebrows knitted. Never had he felt so old. He had second thoughts about going into another café, sure that he would get the same treatment. He went home.

★

Olson stayed at the wheel for a few moments, his head down. He couldn't believe it. No point asking who had killed McGuire. The transparency was starting to scare him. He rubbed his face with both hands, as if washing in cold water, and started the car.

It was now certain, inevitable. Bollington would be arrested for the murder of McGuire, and would tell the police the whole story from the beginning. His forehead had gone clammy. He went back along the dead straight Route Napoléon through Sorges – self-styled truffle-producing capital – and on towards Thiviers. He didn't fancy taking one of the twisty side-roads. He needed symmetry to think.

Did Carter know? He must go and see him, talk to him – he might know more. There were a thousand questions he would have liked to ask Brimmington-Smythe, but the timing had not been right. For one, she was in tears, and for two he wasn't even supposed to know McGuire. McGuire . . . Olson was suddenly moved. Six kids! Shit! And what was now to be done with that dunderhead Bollington?

★

He had arrived early in order to find, as it were, a sheltered spot. He had ended up asking for the times of Mass at the haberdasher's. The woman had seemed to have something particularly Catholic about her which he could not quite put his finger on, and he had not been mistaken. Was it from living amid all these French people, perhaps, that he now had these anthropological reflexes? The haberdasher had told him there was one Mass at Saint-Jean at nine o'clock, and another at Saint-Pierre at eleven. She had hinted that he would do better to go to Saint-Jean, where the congregation was classier. But in any case the same Curé officiated at both. The subject was one that enthused her, and for a moment he thought he would be stuck there all morning, smiling piously as he waited for the reel of thread he had felt obliged to buy and which would be of no use to him. He knew his brother-in-law did not say Mass at Thiviers. So: Saint-Jean or Saint-Pierre it would be. It didn't matter that the church at Saint-Jean drew classier custom and was a more pleasant place, not to mention a good restaurant on the square where he could have had lunch after his religious chore. And anyway, going to Saint-Pierre would mean he could get up later.

There were quite a number of cars parked in front of the church. When he decided to slip inside, he was stopped by a youngish man in farmer's shirt and trousers, who handed him what looked like a religious leaflet and asked him, pleasantly enough, if he would like to read something. Carter mumbled that he would find it difficult, and his accent persuaded the man there was no point insisting. Loads of old ladies piled out of their cars and greeted each other, much as they did on market day in Thiviers. But he still could not see his brother-in-law who, he thought, should have been first to arrive. A gaggle of the old women were talking to a little bald-headed man, even smaller than Carter, who rolled his 'r's when he spoke to them. Then everyone went into the church.

He sat at the back, to the left, hands crossed in front of him. There was no pillar. By way of a crowd there were a dozen or so women, all up front on the right. Carter was sure that, with half the church to himself, he was highly visible from the altar. There were no other men, apart from the one he had just encountered. And he had got all dressed up, too. Feeling absurd in his suit and tie, he started to wonder just why he had come. The story of his life. Putting himself in impossible situations – hellish ones, he nearly said, but the nature of the place restrained him, and he was sorry. Two murders to his name, with a third looming.

The little man now reappeared in a green chasuble with some sort of gilded trappings. Carter didn't understand what was going on. Obviously this man was here to replace his brother-in-law, off sick or on holiday. He announced that Mass would be said for someone who had died and turned to one of the old ladies. Everyone started to murmur. Carter bent his head as if in inspiration, peering up occasionally to observe the church walls eaten away by damp, the few kitsch plaster statues here and there, and the Curé raising his hand like a saint in a Renaissance painting. His brother-in-law was probably off in some other parish. He knew it wasn't he who said Mass in Thiviers, so where? Meanwhile he was stuck here, he could hardly leave in mid-service.

He needed to clear his throat, but didn't dare do that either. Despite himself, the voices echoing in the church inspired in him a kind of fear which he could not have described as 'superstitious', but the sight of faith in the man in green and the old women made him ill at ease. And he was also getting rather bored. When the gospel reading started, he listened.

'"And he said to them in his doctrine, Beware of the scribes, which love to go in long clothing, and love salutations in the marketplaces, and the best seats in the synagogues, and the first rows at feasts; which devour widows' houses, and for a pretence make long prayers. These shall receive greater damnation."' Wonderful. Here was the Book itself telling him he was not wrong to want to be rid of a shit-stirring scribbler. Carter felt his soul uplifted, and he could have been tempted to join the chorus of old ladies at the drop of a hat. To confess. To be washed of his sins.

★

Could the police establish a link between the death of Spencer and that of McGuire? It seemed impossible. Olson hoped Bollington had at least had the taste to use buckshot rather than a bullet, easily identified and traceable straight to the killer. Should Carter be warned? No. Go it alone. He'd had enough of team work. In any case, Carter's game was far from clear. Change country? Could he still do it? Travel catalogues ran through his head. Spain, Portugal? Not far enough. Latin America, India? Oriel would like India: mystical and not expensive. And with all those people, he would be hard to find. He wondered what he had come to do in the Dordogne. India was where he ought to have gone. No, no need to flap. For India, he would first need to sell the house and get rid of all his stuff — and Oriel would ask him what was going on if he suddenly arrived home and said, 'Pack your bags, we're going to India.' The last thought reminded him that he shouldn't trust Oriel: she'd read the first book and was beginning to have doubts about him. When she heard McGuire had been shot by Bollington, she would suspect him, Olson. And come to that, was it Bollington? Wasn't he being too hasty? He was certainly going round in circles, even along this straight road. He needed to stop, he needed a drink. The motion of the car prevented him thinking, his thoughts were in turmoil. He turned left onto the

Ligueux road, a narrower one which made him feel more pro-tected, as if concealed by the trees. He slowed down, turned left again, and then right, at random, with no idea where he was going. He almost needed a pencil and paper to draw up two lists, one of things to do, the other of things not to do, and then by adding them all up perhaps he would arrive at a list of priorities.

★

He nearly committed a faux-pas in the middle of Mass, when all the old ladies stood up to kiss each other. Thinking it was over, he made as if to go to the door. He finally realised it was all part of the ritual, and even now he was still slightly surprised. At least he was glad he had kept himself apart, because the idea of planting kisses on all those crease-worn cheeks sent shivers down his spine.

He breathed deeply while the faithful got back behind their steering-wheels, noticing to his right the terrace of a café he had not spotted earlier. It was too cold to drink outside, so he went in. A couple of steps down into the room and onto some ancient wooden floorboards, grey from repeated washing. A single, vast table ran lengthwise down the room, a bench set along each side. A vile odour hung over the place, and not the usual mix of pastis and brown tobacco. It was more like stepping into someone's home. He cleared his throat noisily to announce his presence, and an old woman appeared – yet another: she might well have been at Mass. In her dark flowered dress of questionable cleanliness, she looked at him with a kind of amusement that defied explanation. She was unbelievably thin, the hands that clasped her stomach forming a pink, blue and white knot of flesh and veins. She wore her hair pulled back. She addressed him with surprisingly elegant diction, so that he wondered if she might not be the lost daughter of some aristocratic or at least upper-middle-class family. He asked for a beer. True, it was a little early, but he deserved it. As he watched her go to the refrigerator at the end of the room to take out a bottle, he realised she was already drunk.

'Were you at Mass?' she asked, setting the bottle on the huge table.

It was clearly the moment to learn a little more about clerical life in the area.

'Yes. You don't go?'

'Oh no. I used to go to Catechism when I was little. But you see, the Curé . . .'

She raised her eyebrows, the amused look still in place.

'Yes?'

'You had to be careful, with that Curé.'

'Which one?'

'He's dead now. It was Abbé Landreau.'

'Really? But the new Curé . . .'

'Abbé Pozzi?'

'Pozzi?'

'Yes, he's Italian. There's no one around here. Not even in France, it seems, to say Mass.'

It was almost as though she was stifling a laugh.

'Oh really? But, er . . . the Abbé,' he said, realising that was how one spoke of curés: 'Abbé Aubier?'

This time, she could not contain herself.

'Oh, him? They call him *tabana* here.'

'I'm sorry?'

'*Tabana*,' she repeated, her forefinger to her temple. 'He's a bit . . . you know.'

'I don't follow.'

'Do you know Aubier?'

'I've heard of him. I thought he was the Curé for the area,' replied Carter, still not entirely sure he understood what a *tabana* was. Perhaps some under-priest in the Catholic hierarchy? He had no idea. In any case, it was puzzling.

'No, no,' she said. 'He would have liked to be, I really wouldn't know. He goes around in a cassock, but that's all. Missed his vocation,' she concluded with a shrug.

At first, Carter refused to believe it. All these years, some loony had been leading him a hellish dance in the name of the Holy Catholic Church, because he was a Protestant, and an atheist to boot. Aided and abetted by his wife Marie and all his in-laws. She must have known her brother was not a priest, and everyone maintained the illusion. Not once had anyone ever told him the cassock was just a disguise. It almost made him feel a bit light-headed. He felt trapped in a gigantic family plot. And Bollington . . . Bollington had this madman to say Mass in his private chapel. This side of it rather made him laugh. But if his brother-in-law wasn't a priest, he was mad, and that changed everything. 'Beware of the scribes, which love to go in long clothing,' Abbé Pozzi had said. It was his brother-in-law who had written the books, his brother-in-law who indeed loved to go in long clothing. He was sure Bollington confessed to him: that was how he knew his story, and Olson's too. As for his own, Marie must have told him, because she knew he had once been up for murder. It was harder to work out how he had come to learn about McGuire's affairs. There was certainly some explanation. The first person to talk to about it all was Bollington. No, rather his wife. With, what was more, the prospect of an agreeable encounter.

'I've got work back there.'

He started. It was the old woman who had spoken. For some minutes he had forgotten he was in a café drinking a beer under the gaze of this somewhat disturbing woman; she had stayed in the same position, without a word.

'Are you absolutely sure that Abbé Aubier . . . that Aubier is not a priest?'

'What did I just tell you? I would hardly make it up, would I?'

'Yes, yes — no, I'm sorry, it's such a surprise, I didn't know.'

She shrugged, took the money for Carter's drink, and retired for a glass of white wine on the quiet.

It was, in one way, wonderful. This hateful man, this liar who spent his life picking on the littleness of others was next on his list. Put not your trust in scribes and long clothing, thought Carter, with a slight modification of Holy Scripture. Indeed. This time it would be he, Carter, who would be preaching the sermon.

★

Extremely slowly, Oriel pushed open the front door. It was her house, this was where she had lived. But each piece of furniture represented a threat. This whole world now seemed foreign to her. She found it hard to believe she had spent all these years within these walls, in a foreign land, and she decided she would now go back, back to England, open a wholefood shop, share a house in Clapham, in Hackney, in Camden, with a yoga teacher and a feng-shui expert, anything to get away from this culture, with its incitement to violence and murder. She would have some pot-plants and that would be plenty.

She had spent the last fortnight with Helen, who lived with Dave. She knew she was perfectly welcome, but she had started interrupting conversations when she came into the sitting-room. She knew that after two weeks her presence had become a weight, despite all her efforts to respect her hosts' privacy. At the table these last evenings, there had been only one subject of conversation — the news of McGuire's death. They were all appalled, and a bit excited as well. After all, he had been shot dead. Murdered, just like in a novel. And so little went on in the

Dordogne in winter, that it would be nice if occasionally life was like a novel.

Nonetheless, Oriel felt less at ease than the others, because she couldn't stop herself suspecting that her own partner might have something to do with it. So she took less part in conversations, limiting herself to a few theories or speculations about what had befallen Johnny, whom she hardly knew anyway. Though she did know he had six children. She knew Laura McGuire, who sometimes came to the workshop to paint. And Oriel, who would have liked to have children, had sometimes caught herself envying the woman.

She kept her ears open, in case Mark came back stealthily. The absence of the car told her he wasn't there, but she was scared. If he had learned she had spent all this time at Helen's . . . She hardly dared picture the scene, the shouting, the plates that would have started flying around Helen's kitchen when he came to fetch her. But about this she was completely wrong: her absence had in no way upset her husband, but perhaps she preferred to nurture the illusion and satisfy the vanity that remained. What remained astonishing was that she had lived with a man all these years without having the slightest inkling of what he really was. A non-violent killer.

She went up to her room, opened the closet and reviewed her wardrobe. There was nothing to retrieve. She was more or less sure that she could never dress like that in Camden, Hackney or Clapham. She was annoyed to have come back here. To retrieve what? Nothing she owned was of the slightest value. What ridiculous instinct had brought her back to this lair where she risked being knocked about?

Then she wondered if she might not find something worth taking among Mark's things. He might perhaps have hidden money, for instance. She began searching frantically, emptying and overturning drawers, scattering clothes on the floor telling herself she was developing a real mania, chucking everything about the rooms of this vile sheep-shed.

At the bottom of the ghastly 1940s cupboard they had bought with the intention of one day painting it with flower patterns there was one big drawer that was never opened. In it she found piles of crumpled old clothes that had once been Mark's. Then it occurred to her that they hadn't been put there to store them, so much as to conceal a secret. She pulled them all out and thrust her hand into the drawer. Her fingers touched something cold and hard. A hunting gun and a box of cartridges covered with labels and markings which meant almost nothing to her.

It was just then that she heard the sound of a car outside.

★

She was not in her bed. He had entered with muffled tread, to surprise her, though wondering if he were not guilty of excessive obedience to the habits of the past, when she should not be disturbed, when the pretence of her illness, her weakness and all the rest had to be kept up.

But he was still astonished not to find her between the sheets. The noise of a lavatory flushing, followed by steps he thought firm. She was coming back. She hadn't heard him – it had been a good idea to come up so stealthily. He watched the porcelain doorknob turn slowly as she opened it.

Carter had flung himself into an armchair and crossed his legs, with the air of someone perfectly calm and self-contained, a sort of shadowy hero able to move about without being heard, appearing when least expected and in the most surprising places. He had come across characters like that in his childhood reading. Staging and performance must have been pretty convincing, because his wife jumped when she saw him and cried:

'Richard! Oh my God! You scared me!'

There was anger in her voice, but she recovered quickly, put a hand to her breast to draw up the collar of her nightdress, then leaned sideways using the back of a chair for support, this time like a nineteenth-century heroine, about to swoon at any moment. She too had encountered this in her reading, but her imitation was far less effective than her husband's performance.

'Oh my God,' she kept whining, pretending to be quite out of breath. 'You gave me such a fright, Richard. Honestly, in my state.'

Then she smiled, as if to soften the scolding, secretly wondering, not without annoyance, why he did not get up to come to her aid and help her to her sick-bed.

He watched her rather haughtily, leaning back with a sarcastic smile, a touch overdone. Realising she could expect nothing from her husband, she moved to the bed with exasperating slowness, then lay down, with movements of her head from side to side, again very exaggeratedly.

'Where have you been, Richard?' she asked in a quavering voice.

'At Mass.'

'What?'

She sat up smartly, straight as a beanpole, jaw clenched, the question slamming about the room like gunshot.

'You heard, Marie. At Mass.'

'What were you doing at Mass?'

'Why, praying, of course,' he replied unctuously, in a reasonably successful imitation of her brother. 'What else would I be doing there, Marie?'

'Very strange, Richard, you've never mentioned this . . . this . . . this interest in faith before. Did you feel the need to talk to God?'

'More or less.'

She frowned.

'What do you mean?'

He didn't reply.

She assumed her dreamy air again, smoothing the sheets with the flat of her hand.

'Did you see anyone we know, Richard?'

'In fact, no.'

'Surely you recognised some people? Jacqueline – you know . . . Jacqueline Dubuission, she goes to Mass in Thiviers every Sunday, and also . . .'

'I didn't go to Thiviers.'

'Oh?'

He said no more. He waited. He saw she had at least noticed something unusual in his attitude without knowing exactly what, or rather she was hesitating to admit it and acknowledge the reason. But he was ready to bet that she had already grasped what this was all about. And a good thing too. He had time, he would wait for her to ask questions. She would certainly beat about the bush wondering if, after all these years of marriage, he had finally realised that her Curé of a brother was just a loony whose crazy habits one forgave.

The look she gave him was gentle, questioning. Still very weak, of course. She saw it would have been better to adopt a more vigorous attitude, because her complainings annoyed him, but she had become incapable of it. Such a well-worn habit . . . It almost frightened her. Because, she was just coming to realise, it was as if she was paralysed, caught in her own game, in this lie which she had more than once believed herself, and which she was now obliged to recognise.

'Why didn't you go to Thiviers? Where did you go?'

'To Saint-Pierre,' he answered. 'Your brother's parish.'

★

If he killed Bollington, it must not be with one of his own guns. So there was no point in going home. Olson decided he needed alcohol, just a little something, perhaps a beer. He was getting tired of driving haphazardly around these country roads. Too many corners. Now it wasn't the straight line, but the very opposite, that was keeping him from thinking.

As he neared a village he didn't recognise because he had never been this way before, he realised when he got to the crossroads by the church that he was at Saint-Pierre. Pulling in, he decided to go and have a drink nearby. He was just closing his car door when a grey car went by and he thought he recognised Carter at the wheel. He thought he must be mistaken. But the sudden appearance made him think again about his one-time accomplice. And again he wondered if he should contact him first. No, Carter would not talk. He didn't have time. Various scenarios of the best way to get rid of Bollington were running through his head, more like films than plans. And all with the same final scene of the fat old bastard writhing in pain in his own blood before expiring. When his imagination took on too much of the cowboy movie, he would pull himself together and make it more realistic. And he decided that Bollington should not know who was killing him — if ever he survived his injuries . . .

★

Bollington was in the grounds, watching his wife and son going off towards the chapel. She was holding Marmaduke's arm. He was in no mind to join them. The priest was there already, waiting for them certainly, because he had seen his car parked in front of the house. Bollington wondered what his wife and son talked to him about. Indeed it may have been the first time he wondered this, with the feeling that he should have done so long ago. Much longer ago. They were walking slowly along the tree-lined path, the uncertain light blurring the details of their clothing: they could have been figures from the distant past appearing to him suddenly, like ghosts. A peaceful image, it scared him somewhat because he felt excluded forever from the calm that surrounded them. Everything seemed frozen, almost as though they would never reach the chapel, set off in the grounds away from the main building. And then the two figures brought him a second scare: for he realised, watching them but unable to hear them, that the words that passed between them had always been incomprehensible to him. It was as though his son suddenly held a mysterious power which he could use against him for all kinds of maleficent designs. It now seemed clear to him that, for all his cowardice and flabbiness, this fat, dreamy, resentful son of his would one day hold everything he needed for revenge. He saw them plotting against him, seeking a way to be rid of him, to humiliate him. He could have started shouting, have gone up to them, have perhaps become violent. But it would all have been in vain. Bollington felt remorse, a feeling so novel that he failed to recognise it. He hadn't wept like this over his lot for such a long time, not, in fact, since his schooldays.

13

'You realise I could suffocate you with your pillow, Marie?'

She was trembling, and her bony hands plucked agitatedly at her white handkerchief. Only this time she wasn't play-acting – she wouldn't have been capable of it. For it was her turn to be afraid, now. He had told her everything, to the point of repeating himself a couple of times. Like a drunkard revelling in his words. He had taken a very real pleasure in revealing that, at long last, he had understood. In justly reproaching her for her lies. In insulting her brother without her being able to answer back. Because he was right and she was wrong. A pleasure he had savoured only too rarely. And he was determined to make a feast of it.

'I could suffocate you with your pillow, Marie,' he repeated once more as he got up from the armchair.

And from the looks that she shot him, he could see she believed that this was no idle threat.

★

It had to be on a Sunday, because fat Albert would be off and not hanging about. Today was Sunday. It couldn't wait a week. Of course there was also the middle of the night. But that wasn't easy, what with the dogs and their bloody barking. People don't bother about barking in the daytime the way they do at night. And beneath this grey sky, thought Olson as he raised his eyes, you sometimes get the impression it's never really day.

At the gate, he stopped. After a moment's thought, he decided to drive on in. His car must not be seen from the road because there was sure to be an investigation. Nor must anyone in the house see him approach.

He wasn't going to talk to Bollington, nor ask him exactly what had happened, or why he had shot McGuire and all the rest of it. He would kill him. With one of his own guns. Olson knew where Bollington kept his arsenal. It was the best way. He couldn't strangle him or stab him, he needed a firearm. If luck was with him, he would find a handgun and make murder look at least vaguely like suicide. That would do. Olson could easily imagine Alexandra Bollington explaining tearfully how her husband was depressed, had recently been having severe black periods. She was the mistress of the doctor, who would confirm that the deceased was taking anti-depressants, and that with such drugs, of course . . .

It was then that he saw him. He was beyond the house, the 'manor' as he called it, and he was watching two distant figures, walking arm-in-arm about a hundred metres away. They were going towards the chapel. And Bollington was following them, his head hanging like a naughty child.

★

She knew he had once been accused of murder. He had told her so himself. And the gleam in his eyes was persuading Marie Carter that she had been wrong to find this detail of his life so exciting. She realised once more, just like the first time she had gone to bed with him, in England before they were married, that the thought had crossed her mind even as she felt his hands on her body: she was sleeping with a man who had killed. Not like a soldier in the heat of battle, but like a murderer. Like a man who has set himself beyond the law, apart, who will never again look at the world in the same way. And she – she gave herself to him. She had never asked for details of the murder he had committed. The technical details. Because she knew he would have refused to give them, even in his cups. He had however spoken of his entanglements with the police, of the grey cells and metal desks, the aggressiveness, the occasional insults. As she listened to these accounts, she felt herself torn between a tender maternal feeling, and an admiration which surprised her. Especially because, even though he always portrayed himself as innocent, she had never believed him. She had never wanted to believe him, secretly preferring to love a skilful murderer who'd got away with it by besting everyone, rather than a victim unable to control his own destiny.

In time, this memory had become something of an abstraction, and he something of a sad little man trotting through the streets of Thiviers. Except that today, at this precise moment, he seemed to have recovered what had excited her so at the time.

He too realised she was regarding him differently, but he couldn't quite fathom just what was putting this gleam in her eye. She was still smiling, but the expression on her face had become somehow firmer. She suddenly looked younger. Even the room no longer gave off its aura of sickness. He felt she was waiting for an explosion of violence with a kind of obscene impatience.

Then, as in a melodrama – because this so very French nineteenth-century house lent itself to such things – they heard the front door open and close again, followed by foot-steps on the stairs. A man's footsteps, rapid and forceful. They exchanged a look. She knew who it was. And she looked at him with a sardonic air because she saw he still hadn't under-stood.

The doctor came into the room without so much as a knock.

'Who said to come in?'

It was Carter who asked the question, the other who was brought up short. It was impossible to tell which surprised him more – the presence of the master of the house, or the tone of his voice.

'I'm sorry, I . . . I came at once. I have news . . .'

'You did not ring. How did you get in?'

Carter knew – he was just eager to embarrass the doctor. A smile played on his face as he wondered whether this man too might not be an impostor, a phoney doctor. After the phoney priest, he was ready for anything.

'The good doctor has a key,' put in Marie.

'Why is that?'

'Don't be silly. I've already told you, you know I'm ill and you're not here all the time, I haven't the strength to get up and go down and all . . .'

'Yes, yes, all right, all right.'

'Is there a problem?' asked the doctor. He had never seen Carter so openly aggressive.

'It's all right, I just said. So – this news of yours?'

'Terrible news,' said the doctor, giving the cliché a theatrical turn. 'Johnny McGuire is dead. Murdered.'

Carter thought he had misheard. He stammered McGuire's name repeatedly. Then he felt as if the air in his lungs was turning to stone. He took a step and fell back into the armchair rather than sitting down in it.

★

When he came into the chapel, Bollington could see neither his wife nor the priest. Marmaduke was off to one side, kneeling before a multicoloured plaster statue of no interest. A worthless, rather sickening devotional ornament, just the kind of thing to satisfy this youth's convoluted tastes. Turning suddenly, the boy stood as if thunderstruck, his eyes protruding, his thick, slightly wet lips quivering. He stared goggle-eyed at his father, his look so fearful that it communicated itself to Bollington without his knowing why.

'Marmaduke?'

'Yes, Daddy?'

'You're not with your mother?'

'No.'

'Where is she?'

'I don't know.'

He was addressing him with a new, almost infantile respect.

'And the Curé's not here?'

'I don't know.'

Bollington frowned:

'What do you mean, you don't know?'

'Er . . . I . . . I . . . I don't know.'

He was now on the verge of tears, though there was nothing new in that. But this time Bollington had not the strength to get angry. He took a few steps towards the altar, utterly distraught. They were hidden behind there, the priest and his wife. Saying not a word. Like two rodents caught by a big cat which has eaten too much to react. He too said nothing. He stood there, stupefied, as though not grasping what was right before his eyes. Marmaduke had started either sobbing or snivelling – in any case making pretty nasty noises with his mouth.

His eyebrows raised, Bollington gave a sigh. He knew she was sleeping with the doctor . . . And now with the priest too. Still in silence, he turned on his heel and made to leave.

As he opened the heavy wooden door he saw Olson, regarding him with a vacant look, saying nothing. Olson had a rifle in his hand and was pointing it at him. His own gun, too – Olson must have got it from the boot of his car.

That was Bollington's last thought. The next instant, he took the blast full in the face.

★

'We know who the murderer is?'

'No, they haven't caught him.'

'How did it happen?'

'We don't know. His wife heard a noise, as she was putting the children to bed. When she came down, she found him dead in the kitchen. Knew him, then?'

'Slightly.'

Carter didn't dare to go on, aware that his wife and the doctor were watching him. Sweat tickled his scalp, and he prayed they would not notice the drop running down his temple.

'We're sure it wasn't suicide?'

'Certain. It was I who examined the body and called the police. Why would he commit suicide, anyway?' the doctor asked slyly, as if in accusation.

'So how was he killed?'

'Gunshots. Two. A hunting rifle.'

It was almost a signature. As he gradually got over the shock, Carter logically deduced that Bollington had shot McGuire. He surely couldn't have imagined that McGuire had written the books? Had he been waiting long for this excuse? Then he heard his wife's voice asking him another question to which he had no answer:

'Richard? What are you thinking?'

★

Bollington was flung backwards by the violence of the shots, his body collapsing onto the chapel floor. Olson then pulled

140

the door closed, sure that no one inside had seen him, and jammed it shut by passing the gun through the two metal handles. They would stay captive inside long enough for him to get away. He must have been mad to come in his own car — too late now for regrets. Luckily he'd had no trouble finding a weapon; he merely had to open Bollington's car boot to find a semi-automatic Manufrance, with an almost full tin of buckshot.

He had run down to the gate and got behind the wheel, and must now have done at least five kilometres without meeting a soul. He took off the gardening gloves, realising he should have done it earlier. At last, he was feeling good. Not shaking, not sweating. He might even stop at the first café for a beer.

How many people would be sorry about Bollington? His wife? No. His son? No. Perhaps big fat Albert. That was quite a laugh. Thinking about it, he ought to have organised things so as to frame Albert for the murder. And he burst out laughing all alone, banging hard on the steering-wheel as if he were slapping his thigh.

★

The atmosphere reminded him somewhat of a social security office. They were sitting at grey metal tables where documents were being photocopied, except that here everyone was in uniform. They were wearing the French képis that the English found a bit exotic and not without charm, because they exuded an air of holidays past, of the *Route Nationale* 7 down to the French Riviera. But their navy blue sweaters had a white band across the chest, like some designer rugby shirt. Everything in the room was either navy blue or grey. Even him, with his grey hair and his double-breasted navy blue suit.

When they had knocked at the door two days ago, they had shown a politeness which Carter had thought excessive.

Panic-stricken, however, he had turned his back to them and showed them in, in what might have seemed an offhand way. Then in somewhat honeyed tones he had asked the gendarmes if they would like a drink. They had refused, still politely, but a bit curtly nonetheless. They had come slowly into the sitting-room, looking up and to left and right, like prospective buyers sent round by the estate agent.

Then they started asking him about McGuire. 'Did you know him?' – answer: 'Not very well, I met him sometimes at friends.' He didn't hide that he knew what had happened, and it was almost in triumph that he was able to explain how: 'My wife is very ill, and she has the same doctor as the McGuires. He told us the dreadful news the last time he was here.' He realised the vocabulary he was using was clearly rather pompous, but knew he would be forgiven because he was a foreigner, and in any case the flowery words helped reassure him, although he couldn't explain why. He had the impression that sticking to purely official statements would somehow protect him from other, more personal questions. In the same manner, he explained that he had not been sufficiently close to Johnny – sorry, with John McGuire – to know whether the latter had any personal enemies.

In the middle of the interview, a groaning could be heard from the floor above. The gendarmes glanced up and, for the first time, they looked at him a bit suspiciously, with raised eyebrows.

'My wife,' he said. 'She is ill, as I told you. Will you excuse me while I go up and see?'

They let him go with a wave of the hand. As he went up he said, over his shoulder:

'I shan't be long.'

She had reassumed her role of patient. He couldn't believe it. But even if it exasperated him, he didn't have the strength to start a scene, especially not with the gendarmes waiting for him downstairs.

'What is it, Richard?' she asked in her quavering voice.

'It's nothing, Marie, you rest now.'

What else could he do than speak the same old lines? It had been going on for twenty years.

'Who's downstairs, Richard?'

'It's the gendarmes.'

'You're not in trouble, I hope, Richard?'

The old bitch. She must be aching for them to have come to take him away.

'No, Marie,' he replied, 'it's nothing.'

But anger restored his strength. It was not the first time he had been in this situation, and he could at last conclude that he had a survival instinct which came into play suddenly and which she would one day pay for, when the occasion arose.

Going back down, at the fourth stair, he wondered if the gendarmes had read the books in which he figured, and had recognised him. The idea chilled him, and he thought he felt a drop of sweat trickling down his worn skin, under his shirt, between his shoulder blades. Although his hands were clammy, he tried not to wipe them on his trousers. He was invited to call in at the gendarmerie. He protested half-heartedly, on the grounds of having nothing much to add. But they said his statement must be taken as part of the enquiry. He had wanted to ask, 'Why? Are you trying to write a book?' but had the good taste to restrain himself.

★

There now remained only himself and Carter. And as he spelled this out, a thought struck him. What if it was Carter who wrote the book? Or, to be precise, the books. No. He refused to believe it. It was Carter who had raised the alarm,

143

although that didn't mean much. McGuire could not have written them, basically because, much as Olson disliked the conclusion, it must be recognised that he was too honourable for that kind of thing. Time for a little lucidity. Carter, now, was cultivated and sedentary enough to sit down and write. Strange, really – they had almost come to forget the business of the book. Coming down to it, Olson reckoned that if Bollington had killed McGuire, it was basically because he had wanted to. And while he was at it, he wondered if the same hadn't been true of him regarding Bollington.

Olson now felt a certain lassitude. He had after all worked hard, and decided he should now take one thing at a time. He remembered there was beer – good and strong, too – in his refrigerator, and with any luck a football match on television. And perhaps a little joint, to round everything off? It was for all these reasons that he had wanted to live in the country. He decided that in the coming weeks he would get a satellite dish. It would disfigure the house a bit, but what the hell.

Coming into the drive leading to his cottage, a cloud appeared on his horizon. The car parked out front told him that Oriel was back. It wasn't that he recognised the car, which she had obviously borrowed from a girlfriend. He could easily picture her going through the house, no doubt looking for cash.

Annoyed to have had such negative thoughts, he now had the feeling the worst was over. A feminine presence, after all . . . He could make an effort, a reconciliation scene and a little self-criticism, not allowing himself to upbraid her at all.

He got out of the car and slammed the door. He smiled as he approached the porch, thinking he needed nothing more, for a peaceful, contented existence, than this halfway comfortable sheep-shed.

★

He had carefully rehearsed what he would say to them. Vague answers. Words devoid of meaning, his tone perfectly friendly. He would talk to the gendarmes the same way he had talked to his wife for years.

He had already waited a good five minutes where he sat, perhaps even ten. He could hear them talking, too fast for him really to grasp what about.

It was then that he saw them. He thought it was a dream. Alexandra Bollington, together with his brother-in-law, had come through the door. They hadn't noticed him as they stood in the hall, heads bowed, clearly upset. A gendarme asked them into the office. Carter stared vacantly at a map of the Dordogne on the wall. Why his brother-in-law, with Bollington's wife, and not Bollington himself? The gendarme came in and interrupted his thoughts:

'Did you know Monsieur Bollington?'

Monsieur Bollington, he'd said, it was almost comical. Then Carter frowned. Had he spoken of Bollington in the past tense? It might partly explain what he had just seen. Had his wife killed him? Abetted by the brother-in-law? That would be too perfect.

'I see Bollington now and then,' he said, careful to use the present tense. 'Our relations are perfectly cordial.'

He gave an amused little smile, as if to say he felt indulgent towards the man while remaining far more reserved himself, before adding: 'He's quite a character.'

He then adopted a convincingly quizzical look, and asked:

'But why . . . I . . . I don't follow . . . I hope nothing has happened to Bollington.'

He raised his eyebrows and tilted his head to one side.

'He is dead.'

Carter was dumbfounded. Then, this rather brutal way of

giving him the news put him on his guard. These things were usually done more tactfully. Perhaps it was because they suspected him.

'Oh God! But . . . ! But . . . ! That's dreadful, I had no idea. And . . . and . . .'

The gendarme looked at some papers scattered on the desk.

'And how did it happen?'

'He was shot dead, two shots.'

Carter said nothing. Two shots. Like McGuire. So it wasn't Bollington who had killed Johnny. It was Olson: he must have made up his mind to eliminate everybody. He refused to believe it was a coincidence. He had even forgotten the possibility that the culprit might be his own brother-in-law.

In a neutral voice, Carter asked:

'Has the . . . murderer . . . been caught?'

'No, but he will be. And there's a third murder.'

'A third?'

They surely could not have made the connection with the killing of Spencer. It was impossible. Unless someone had talked. There was only one person who could have. And that was when the man asked him:

'Do you know Olson?'

★

'Oriel! Oriel!'

He opened the door. Oriel was there, waiting for him.

She had his gun and was pointing it at him. At first he thought it was a joke. He was quite fond of repetitive jokes. But this wasn't a joke. He too received two blasts of buckshot in the face.

For some moments she remained aghast at the sight, as if unable to take it in. As if overcome by the effectiveness of the instrument she held in her hands, which had turned a dream into reality.

He had gone over backwards, his body across the threshold. Oriel remained in front of him, stock-still, but the hardening of her face showed that stupefaction was yielding to reflection. She was chewing her lip, with an intent look. Very, very slowly she lowered the gun, to lean it against the wall. She took a step forward, thought about dragging the body into the house by the legs. Then she stopped, turned and went to the kitchen.

Annoyed to see he hadn't done the washing-up for days, she put on the yellow rubber gloves by the sink. Then she went to the drawer for the big butcher's knife.

Returning to the body, she undid the shoelaces, took the shoes off, and stuck her hands into them. She then went and rubbed the soles in the mud outside, returned to dirty the floor of the room, and put the shoes back on him. She broke a lamp, and overturned chairs and the table. As she set about smashing things with the thoroughness of a good housewife, she thought about the immediate and the not-so-immediate future. She said to herself, softly:

'Why, I do believe I shan't have to leave after all.'

She went up to the wall, clenched her teeth, and banged her forehead against it, following that with a sharp blow to her cheek with the handle of the knife. Doubling over and getting her breath back, she waited for the pain to turn into a feeling of heat, and did it all again. She went to look at herself in the bathroom mirror. With a sigh, she decided it wasn't bad, but not yet dramatic enough. So, with a hardiness that surprised her, she hit herself a third time. Her cheekbone began to swell up, red at first, then slowly turning blue as the eye closed. A blow on the lip too? Painful, but necessary. She did it. She spat a little blood, and the sight of the liquid reminded her of what she still had to do. Going to her husband's body, the knife still in her yellow-gloved hand, she squeezed his inert fingers

147

around the handle. Her courage ever-increasing now, she gave herself a cut on the collar-bone. The result was more than satisfactory. She walked about the room. Blood splattered everywhere.

Then she went to the telephone and found the directory. The number she wanted was in the first few pages. Then, as if from a great distance, she heard her own voice saying, in hesitant and strongly accented French:

'I've killed my husband, he told me he had killed a man, Johnny McGuire, and he went mad, he tried to kill me.'

★

'Olson?'

Carter said the name barely audibly. He was having trouble swallowing. He imagined the author of the books moving on to his next phase: having revealed their secrets, determined now to kill them one by one. He was the only one left. He would go home, pack his bags and leave. Anywhere. Spain. No, further, Portugal. No, wait, what was he saying, that was him all over, forever thinking small. He would go to South America at least, or to Vietnam for instance. The worst, or nearly so, was not knowing what the other three had revealed, and to whom, before they died.

He heard a commotion in the hall behind him and turned. The door of the office had stayed open all this time. He saw a woman come in, her face bruised and swollen. She was accompanied by three gendarmes.

The one questioning Carter got up and, with a muttered 'Excuse me' to no one in particular, went out to the others and asked, 'Well?'

Carter did not know that this was Olson's wife, whom he had never met. But he overheard one of the men saying:

'This is Madame Olson, back from the hospital. We'll take her statement.'

'Fine, hang on, I'll be right there.'

The man came back into the office where Carter still waited:

'I'm sorry,' he said, 'I'll have to ask you to come back another day. But you didn't answer my question. Did you know him?'

Struck by an idea he thought excellent, Carter replied:

'No, I only knew him by sight. But I believe he used to work for Bollington.'

There, just like that, he had at least established a link between the two, which was bound to be confirmed by Bollington's wife.

Timidly, Carter asked:

'Was it his wife who killed him?'

'I can't talk to you about it.'

The gendarme shrugged, before adding:

'If so, it was in any case self-defence.'

Self-defence. What a wonderful idea, Carter thought. He was aware of the gendarme saying:

'You can go home for the moment.' He very nearly asked, 'Are you sure?', but didn't. He got up with some difficulty and left the room almost backwards, nodding at the man in uniform. He was done in. The sky over Thiviers was pearly, the first time he'd seen that. Carter felt torn between a sense of profound security and a certain heaviness which slowed his step. Olson had been killed by his wife. Was that why the books had been written, to kill them all? It made no sense. Was it Olson's wife who had written the novels? Who had ended up choosing, for her husband, a gun, quicker, more effective? No, it wasn't Olson's wife. He couldn't really have said why. Perhaps because she couldn't have known that he too had committed murder, so long ago, in England. Still . . . He no longer believed any secret. Everybody was talking about everybody else. He was suddenly struck by the penultimate thing that had occurred to him: it had never crossed his mind that the author could be a woman.

★

'Now that he's dead, we can live together, Alexandra.'

'No.'

Michel Beynac was rather taken aback by this brief reply:

'But why, I . . .'

'I'm in love,' she said with a mocking smile.

This time he was almost certain she was having him on. But needing confirmation, he burst into somewhat forced laughter. Her expression had not altered.

'So who's the lucky man?' he asked, his tone still jocular.

'Quite honestly, it's none of your business. But it amuses me to tell you.'

No doubt about it, she was quite serious, and he was quite taken aback. This woman, right here before him was, she said, 'in love'.

'I've decided I'd like to live with the husband of your mistress.'

This was very far from clear. She saw he was awaiting further details but didn't dare ask, and she decided to make him wait a little longer.

'Not sure which mistress I mean?'

He did not reply. But the tone was no longer jocular.

'Marie Carter,' she said finally.

He frowned. Had he misheard? Was she really telling him she was breaking off their relationship because she was in love with Carter? In love with Carter, it seemed like a contradiction in terms.

'Yes,' she went on, 'we're leaving here, Richard Carter and I. I don't know our destination yet, but that's almost irrelevant.'

'And how long ago did you decide this?'

'He still doesn't know.'

'Oh really? So what makes you think he'll agree?'

'I've noticed he fancies me. After that, it's simple. Anyway, no one ever refuses me anything. You might as well do the same with his wife.'

'And how do you know she's my mistress?'

'Her brother told me. He's my lover too, and anyway you ought to know that round here everybody knows everything about everybody else.'

'The priest?'

'Yes, well, the loony who takes himself for one. My poor husband, God rest his soul, never realised he was a nutter in a cassock. But very handsome, plenty of body tone.'

Michel Beynac perceived in this last remark a not over-flattering hint regarding himself. He raised his eyebrows and, with a cruel little sneer, counter-attacked:

'And is it for old Carter's muscles that you're running off with him?'

'I've read things about him, and I like his character. Anyway, I've got complex tastes.'

Michel Beynac emptied his glass, then went out to his car without a goodbye, without a single word. For which Alexandra Bollington was almost grateful.

Driving away from the manor, he thought over what his former mistress had said, and remembered that Marie Carter had a lot of money.

★

Coming into the house, he realised at once that it was empty.

151

It was as if the very furniture breathed more easily. The room had an unusual lightness.

He had stayed out all day, going from bar to bar, dawdling, not drunk, just relieved.

Olson's wife was being held for twenty-four hours. The Périgueux police were now in charge of the investigation, and had established it was indeed self-defence, and that Olson was guilty of murdering both McGuire and Bollington.

Carter was personally convinced that it was half unfair, but as they were dead it no longer mattered.

It was Alexandra Bollington who had given him the details in the course of a telephone call that was surprising on more than one count.

He knew now that they had all been wrong from the start, that it was a woman who had written the books, as he had guessed, on leaving the gendarmerie. But it was neither Norma Olson, alias Oriel, nor Alexandra Bollington.

It was a woman who listened at doors and glued her ear to floorboards, a woman in whom he had confided, who had collected the confidences of those two great sources of human wisdom, religion and science – her brother, and her doctor, both of whom slept with just about everybody. A woman who had no motive apart from curiosity, resentment, and the pure pleasure she got from the opportunity to do harm, which was a lot in itself and, in any case, quite sufficient.

He glanced at the fireplace and the cold, grey ashes, the Archangel Gabriel still furious on his metal backplate.

He had gone slowly up to Marie's room, opened the door, and gone straight to the small table, where a note lay on a pile of papers. In it, Marie explained that he had forty-eight hours to pack his bags, that she intended to divorce him and start life afresh with a fine man, her doctor Michel Beynac, who had shown his solicitude yet again by placing her brother in the psychiatric hospital at Montpon.

Carter read it all with an amused smile, thinking that for once she was wrong to imagine she could get to him.

Then he peered at the pages piled next to the letter. Judging from their thickness, there must be two or three hundred of them. It was a manuscript. She could hardly have forgotten it. The pages had been left there for him to find. He turned the title page and read the first paragraph:

Seated in his leather armchair with a glass in his hand, he gazed dolefully at the flames in the fireplace. Three logs lay burning, on top of them a book. The fire flared as the flames licked at the pages.